C000164762

PRICED TO KILL

CATHERINE BRUNS

∿

PRICED TO KILL

by

CATHERINE BRUNS

∿

Second Edition

Copyright © 2021 by Catherine Bruns

Cover design by Yocla Designs

All rights reserved. Without limiting the rights under copyright reserved above, no part of this publication may be reproduced, stored in or introduced into a retrieval system, or transmitted, in any form, or by any means (electronic, mechanical, photocopying, recording, or otherwise) without the prior written permission of both the copyright owner and the above publisher of this book.

This is a work of fiction. Names, characters, places, brands, media, and incidents are either the product of the author's imagination or are used fictitiously. The author acknowledges the trademarked status and trademark owners of various products referenced in this work of fiction, which have been used without permission. The publication/use of these trademarks is not authorized, associated with, or sponsored by the trademark owners.

❀ Created with Vellum

ACKNOWLEDGMENTS

For this book, I relied heavily on assistance from professionals in the police, real estate, and medical fields. Special thanks to retired Troy Police Captain Terrance Buchanan, who always has the answers I need. My former manager Mary Peyton never fails me or the real estate market. Stephanie DelSignore, R.N., provided much needed information in the medical field. To beta readers Kathy Kennedy, Krista Gardner, Constance Atwater, and Krista Clark—what would I do without you? For my husband Frank, who may just have the toughest job of anyone— living with me. And as always, a profound thank you to publisher Gemma Halliday and her fabulous staff who always make my books better.

CHAPTER ONE

"Good morning, Forte Realty."

"May I speak to Cindy York, please?"

I didn't recognize the deep, male voice on the other end, but that wasn't unusual. As a real estate agent, it was my job to assist clients and deal with inspectors and various mortgage brokers. The strange voice could belong to any of those.

Hopeful, I grabbed a pen and notepad from my desktop. "This is Cindy. How may I assist you?"

"Cindy, it's Ben Steadman. How are you?"

A giant knot formed in the pit of my stomach. Ben was the older brother of my friend, Paul, who had committed suicide twenty-five years earlier. Even after all this time, I still found myself biting my lower lip to force back tears.

My voice sounded shaky to my own ears. "Fine and yourself?"

There was a brief silence. "It's been a long time."

"Yes, it has." I knew now why he was calling but let him broach the subject.

Ben cleared his throat. "I didn't see your name on the list of RSVPs for the dinner tomorrow night."

"Ah, no. I can't make it." It was a little white lie, but I couldn't help myself. My twenty-fifth high school reunion was being held the following evening at the Steadman home. Ben's wife, Michelle, had been a former classmate of mine and Paul's. When I had first received the invitation in the mail, I'd been somewhat excited about the event. That reaction had changed quickly when I found out the reunion was to be held at Ben's house—the same home where Paul had killed himself. I hadn't set foot in the stunning Victorian mansion since that horrible day when I'd been the one to discover his lifeless body. And I had no intention of doing so again.

Ben's voice was gentle. "I know how you feel. But I really think you should come. Paul would have wanted you there. And remember, there's the time capsule your class buried at graduation. We'll be opening it tomorrow night. Surely you'd like to see that?"

A tear rolled down my cheek before I could stop it. "I'm sorry, Ben. I don't think I can do it."

He sighed. "Well, there is another matter I'd like to speak with you about."

At this point, I welcomed any change of subject. "Of course."

"I'm retiring and selling my practice." Ben was a prominent attorney who specialized in matrimonial law, like his deceased father had before him. As the only surviving child, he'd inherited both the business and his parents' lavish home. Paul had wanted to become a doctor. I wondered...

"Cindy? Are you still there?"

I forced myself back to the present. "Sorry, Ben, my mind was wandering. Congratulations on your retirement. Michelle must be thrilled. I haven't seen her in ages."

"Thanks, we're both excited about it. We own a condo in Bermuda that we'll be moving to, so we're looking to sell our house. I knew you were in the industry and wondered if you could assist us."

My heart started to thump against the wall of my chest at a fervent rate. If I could sell the Steadman property, it would do wonders for my income, not to mention the prestige I would gain in the real estate market. "Thank you, I'm flattered. I don't know what to say."

"Say you'll come to the reunion tomorrow night," Ben said. "Bring your husband and I'll give you both a personal tour of the house."

"Greg's out of town on business."

"Well, bring a friend then. And I'm sure Michelle would love to see you. Don't forget to bring a listing contract, too." He must have placed his hand over the receiver because his voice became muffled for a moment. "Cindy, my secretary is here. I have a client on the other line. Call me if you have any questions. I'll see you tomorrow night. The reunion starts at six."

"Ben—I—hello?"

I was talking to dead air. With a sigh, I placed the office phone back into its cradle and pushed my long, dark hair back from my face. Now what was I going to do? I needed this sale and badly. But at what cost?

I whirled my swivel office chair around and stared out the second-story window of my office. It was a Friday morning in late July. I reached over and pulled the venetian blind down. It was a shame to cover the spectacular view of the nearby lake with the sun shimmering on its surface, but the heat beat through the floor-length glass window at a furious pace.

I checked my phone and saw that the temperature was already hovering around ninety degrees outside. Weather in Upstate New York was often unpredictable. Next week it might be sixty degrees and rainy. But the news weathermen had warned that we were in for a scorcher of a weekend ahead.

The room and the entire building were silent with the

exception of the clicking heard from the overhead ceiling fan.
Central air-conditioning kept the building at a comfortable
level, even on days like this, but Jacques Fortes, my best friend
and now-recent boss had been grumbling all week about the
high cost of utilities.

My cell phone buzzed from my desk, and I glanced down at
the screen before I picked it up. "Hi, honey."

"Hey." My husband Greg's voice floated through the phone.
"How's my sweetheart doing today?"

I clutched the phone tightly to my ear. "Fine, but I miss you.
Promise me this is the last trade show for a while."

He chuckled. "I think I can arrange that." Greg and I had
been married for eighteen years. He'd recently been promoted
to a sales management position at a local automotive company,
which required him to do a bit more traveling. The raise had
been a huge boost to our income, but I hated sleeping alone.

"Will you be home tomorrow?" I asked.

"I think so, but it'll be pretty late."

"Then I'll wait up for you. It looks like I might be attending
my high school reunion after all."

Silence ensued. "Cin, didn't you say that was being held at
the house where—"

I cut him off. "Yes. I haven't decided if I'm going or not, but
Ben's retiring, and they're moving away. They'd like me to list
their home, so if I want the contract, it's kind of a no-brainer to
attend the event."

"Baby, this is your call. Don't do anything you're not
comfortable with."

As I listened to the sound of Greg's voice, I longed for his
strong, powerful arms around me. "I can't wait till you get
home."

"Me either. Send the kids to my mother's tomorrow night.
We'll have a special homecoming, just the two of us, like when
we celebrated our anniversary last month."

I giggled. "I still don't remember much about that night."

"Well, I remember *every* detail. Just you, me, and the strip-tease you performed for my eyes only. God, that was fantastic."

Heat flooded my face, and I shut my eyes tight. "Oh, wow. I must have been really drunk."

"Yeah. It was great."

"Cindy?" I heard Jacques' impatient voice call.

"Greg, I have to go. Call me later?"

"Sure thing, baby. Love you."

"Love you too."

I clicked off just as Jacques entered my office. Like me, Jacques was in his early forties. He was an attractive man with a muscular build, thick blond hair, and Prada eyeglasses that he wore over sharp, green eyes that missed nothing and were fixated on me now. He folded his arms across his chest and tapped his foot.

"What's wrong?"

He pointed at one of the matching easy chairs situated in front of my desk. "*That's* what's wrong. Which one of your clients broke the arm?"

I opened my mouth in surprise. "What have you been doing? Inspecting the furniture after I leave every night?"

Jacques sank into the other dark blue, overstuffed chair. "Listen, darling, I'm stuck with the bills, so don't take it personally. You're acting more and more like Ed every day."

Ed Kapinski was Jacques' spouse. They'd been married for over a year. Ed was Jacques' total opposite—a quiet, balding man who looked a bit like the actor Ed Harris. He was employed as manager for a prominent restaurant in the area. Also unlike Jacques, he only spoke when he had something important to say.

"I'm guessing that's not a compliment?"

Jacques snorted. "That man could drive me to drink some

days." He reached out and patted the lumpy chair arm. "I bet I know who did this too."

I shifted in my seat. "I don't know what you mean."

"Oh, yes, you do. You let Barney sit in that chair yesterday, didn't you?"

I sighed. Like a bloodhound, Jacques never missed anything. "What was I supposed to do? Make him sit on the floor?"

"Cin, the man is over five-hundred pounds. The floor is about the *only* thing he can't break. Maybe."

"He's a client. And you always said that the client is king."

"King, yes. But he weighs more than the entire royal family." Jacques took his eyeglasses off and polished them on his shirt before putting them back on again. "I have to conserve wherever I can. Sales have not been good this past month."

That was an understatement. I'd only had two closings and nothing scheduled on the books. Three clients of mine were currently looking for houses—Barney Drake included—but they hadn't found anything yet. "The market will turn around soon. You'll see."

"It had better," he said dryly. "What we need right now is a couple of mansions to boost our sales."

Oh boy. I immediately lowered my eyes to the desk.

Jacques watched me suspiciously. "Cynthia Ann, you're hiding something. Out with it."

"I don't know what you're talking about."

"Please, darling, don't insult my intelligence. I know you, remember? You'll never have a poker face."

I twisted a ballpoint pen between my fingers. "I received a call from Ben Steadman today. He's interested in having me list his house."

Jacques' eyes bugged so far out of his head I was afraid he might lose his balance and topple out of the chair. "*The* Ben Steadman? The prominent divorce attorney?"

"Close your mouth. You're starting to drool."

"And isn't his wife a choreographer or something like that for the Jets' cheerleaders?"

"She used to be. I read somewhere she still consults on an as-needed basis. I graduated high school with Michelle. She was a fantastic cheerleader herself and even made the squad for the Dallas Cowboys but didn't stay."

"Why not?"

I took a sip from the Starbucks cup on my desk. "She was pregnant."

Jacques sniffed. "Well, that must have put a wrinkle in things."

"Hmm." I had nothing against Michelle personally, but we hadn't run in the same circle of friends or kept in touch over the years. For some reason, I was on their annual Christmas card list, which always included a photo and details of what the family had been up to during the past year. It was a bit contrived for my taste.

When she'd first met Ben at a party, she'd immediately dug her claws in and had never loosened her grip. Ben was three years our senior and had been attending a local college. When she wound up pregnant, Ben had done the honorable thing and married her. From what I'd learned over the years, she was a devoted mother to their only child and the perfect wife to a prestigious attorney. I'd read about some of the fabulous dinner parties she'd hosted over the years and knew she did a great deal of charity work as well.

Jacques leaned forward across my desk. "There's something you're not telling me here. Why aren't you more excited about listing this house? You're been dying for a deal like this. And, frankly, so have I."

I swallowed hard. "It's the same house my friend Paul committed suicide in."

Jacques was silent for a few seconds, and then he reached

across the desk to squeeze my hand. "I'm sorry, dear. I had no idea."

For years, I had been trying to block out the mental picture of Paul's lifeless body that day. Most of the time I was successful. We'd been best pals since kindergarten. Our lifestyles had been different, but that hadn't mattered. While Paul's family was rich and powerful, my father had died when I was a baby, and my mother and I lived on a shoestring budget. Despite his family's stature, Paul had never put on airs around me or made me feel I wasn't good enough.

Jacques interrupted my thoughts. "Everything okay?"

I was touched by the look of concern in his eyes. "After all these years, I still wake up sometimes in the middle of the night and ask myself why. Why him?"

He shrugged. "I don't have the answer to that question, love. That's something only Paul will ever know." He examined my face. "So, what do you think? I'll go with you to meet the Steadmans if that will help."

"I haven't been in the house since that day." I stopped to draw a deep breath. "It would be difficult for me. And there's more."

Jacques' face was pained. "Now what?"

"Tomorrow night is my twenty-fifth high school reunion. I had planned on going until I found out that Michelle and Ben were hosting it—at their house, that is. Now Ben has asked me to attend especially. And he wants me to bring a contract with too."

A small squeal escaped from Jacques' mouth, and he high-fived me. "Girlfriend, we've *got* to have that listing. I'll be your guest for the reunion."

I wrinkled my nose. "You hate reunions. Didn't you tell me you'd rather be tarred and feathered instead of being forced to attend one?"

"Well, yes," Jacques admitted, "but I was talking about mine, not yours." His eyes searched mine beseechingly. "*Please*, Cin.

We need this. When's the last time I ever asked you for anything?"

He had me on that one. I'd started my real estate career at Hospitable Homes over three years ago. An incident a few months back had left me scrambling for gainful employment, and Jacques came to my rescue, only too happy to provide me with the opportunity to join his new brokerage. Besides Greg, he was the only man I'd ever been able to count on in my life.

Having no choice, I relented. "Okay. I'll have to see if my mother-in-law can watch the twins tomorrow night though. Darcy's going to a concert with a friend, so I don't have anyone else to ask."

"I'll drag Ed over there if I have to," Jacques said grimly. "Does this event require formal wear?"

"Semi-formal," I said. "I have a silk dress I was thinking about wearing."

"I'll wear a black suit." Jacques tapped his pen on my desk. "That mansion is a gold mine. I may even have a client who's already interested. This is just what we need to save our summer. I'd hate to have to let one of the other agents go, but it might be coming to that."

"But we all work off of commission," I argued. "We don't get paid unless there's an actual sale. So why would you have to get rid of someone?"

"All the overhead costs," Jacques explained. "If this keeps up, I'm going to have to find a smaller building too. While I may not be paying out weekly salaries, there are other related expenses. *For Sale* signs, postage, utilities, the office computers, and," he pointed to the broken chair again, "furniture repairs."

"Okay, point well taken. The reunion starts at six o'clock. How about picking me up about fifteen minutes before?"

"Sounds like a plan. I will be your perfect escort and chauffeur." He stood and gave an exaggerated bow. "Nothing will mess this sale up for us, my dear. I guarantee it."

CHAPTER TWO

*T*he doorbell rang, and I braced myself. *Okay, be nice. You can do this.*

Before I could reach the front door, my twins, Stevie and Seth, bounded past me down the stairs with our dog, Rusty, barking at their heels.

Stevie flung the door open and wrapped his arms around the waist of the elderly woman standing there. "Hi, Grandma!"

Helen York smiled broadly as she stooped down to give both of the boys a hug. "Hello, darlings! How I've missed you!"

Seth's face was puzzled. "But we just saw you last week. There wasn't time to miss us."

"Don't be rude," I admonished him.

Helen handed a bag to Stevie who ran into the kitchen with it. She glanced briefly at me. "Oh, hello, Cindy."

"Hi, Helen. Thanks for coming."

She ignored my comment and focused her attention on the twins. "I guess it's just you and me tonight, huh? Have you eaten?"

"We had dinner," Stevie said, breathless from his sprint. "Spaghetti and salad."

"Well, you let Grandma know if you want me to fix you anything. You're so skinny. I bet you haven't had a decent meal in weeks."

I rolled my eyes toward the ceiling. Helen York's snide comments were plentiful, especially when directed at me. She's a sophisticated, attractive woman in her late sixties or so with short, gray hair perfectly coiffed and piercing blue eyes. She never divulges her true age, and even Greg has admitted he isn't positive how old she is. From the first day we'd met, I hadn't measured up in her eyes and knew I'd never be good enough for her son. My children were a different matter though. She thought the sun rose and set on them. Helen was their only surviving grandparent, and I was grateful she doted on them, despite our differences.

Stevie and Seth were typical eight-year-olds, full of energy that I envied. Both resembled their father, with light brown hair and sparkling blue eyes. They were imps who knew no boundaries. As of late, they were obsessed with the Harry Potter movies and books. Helen had recently chastised me for buying them. A few months ago they'd been watching *The Sopranos* reruns on the sly until Greg had caught them and finally put a password lock on that particular television channel. Overall, I felt that Harry Potter was a significant improvement.

Rusty, our cocker spaniel, quickly attached himself to Helen's pant leg while the boys howled with laughter.

"Cynthia." Helen's face was crimson as she pushed the excited dog away. "Will you please teach this creature to behave?"

"He wants to make babies," Stevie shouted.

Seth furrowed his brow. "He's the word that begins with an *H*. My friend Tyler told me all about it but I can't remember now. They said it on *The Sopranos*."

Helen's expression quickly turned from one of annoyance to .horror. "What word?"

Stevie turned to me for assistance. "Do you know what the word is, Mom?"

Good grief. "Hungry," I said hurriedly. "Rusty's just hungry. You can give him some treats later."

Seth shook his head. "I don't think that's the word. I heard Dad say it to you once too. I passed your bedroom to get a drink of water late at night. Then Dad..."

Oh boy. "Okay, then." I forced a smile to my lips. "You two need to get upstairs to take your showers. Let's move."

The look of shock on Helen's face probably mirrored my own. She stood there, glowering, not saying a word. I turned my back on her and guided the boys toward the stairs.

It was times like this when I wished the earth would swallow me up whole. "Chop-chop, now. Hurry up so you can play games with Grandma later. And behave yourselves." I gave each one of them a kiss and added a gentle push before I sent them on their way upstairs.

"Rusty needs a girl dog to make babies with." Stevie shouted as he ran up the stairs behind his brother.

I turned around and braced myself to meet Helen's disapproval again, but she had already disappeared into the kitchen. I watched as she removed cheese, crackers, and apples from her tote bag. It wasn't like my cupboards were bare, but Helen always managed to find fault with everything of mine.

I forced politeness into my voice. "Helen, it was nice of you to bring food, but I have plenty of fruit in the fridge and snacks up in the cupboards."

She cut her eyes to my face then they dropped to focus on my outfit. "Didn't you say you were going to a fancy event tonight?"

"Yes, a high school reunion at the Steadman mansion. I went to school with Michelle Steadman."

Helen pursed her lips. "Isn't that outfit a little young for you?"

I sucked in some air and gazed down at the cocktail dress I was wearing. I knew I'd put on a couple of pounds lately, and it was a bit snug, but I thought I still looked good. I'd worn it for our anniversary dinner last month, and my husband had been full of compliments. Then again, even a burlap bag would have turned Greg on lately.

What's wrong with my dress? The neckline was a bit on the low side but not impractical. Not that it mattered though. It could have been a nun's habit, and Helen would still find fault because I was the one wearing it.

Mercifully, Jacques' car horn sounded from outside at that moment. I picked up my black evening bag and pressed it under my arm. "I shouldn't be any later than eleven."

Helen made a small snort that she directed toward the apple she was slicing. "Who's taking you?"

"Jacques."

That brought about an even larger snicker. "How ironic that I happen to be slicing fruit right now. Have a nice time, dear."

I clenched my fists at my sides in an effort to restrain myself from lunging for her throat. She could say what she wanted about me, but my best friend was a different matter. Still, I forced myself to take the high road. Sort of. "Do be careful with that knife, Helen. Oh, wait, I forgot. You don't bleed."

Helen was so surprised by my comment that she almost dropped the knife. I hurried to the front door and heard her yell something as I slammed the door behind me.

I ran to Jacques' convertible and slid into the front passenger seat.

He glanced at me quizzically. "What's wrong?"

"Just drive," I ordered. "As far away from here as possible."

"Ah," Jacques gestured at Helen's Chevy with a smile. "It's the mother-in-law who comes airmailed straight from hell." He hit the gas pedal at full force while I grabbed the door handle in a panic.

"Jeez, slow down," I said.

Jacques ignored my plea. "I have a contract with me and some comps for Ben and Michelle to look over. You know that Victorian over on Genesee Way?"

I nodded. "Didn't that just sell?"

"Yep," Jacques said. "Last month. It's slightly larger than Ben's but went for close to two million. This deal could work miracles for the agency."

"No pressure, right?" I stifled a groan and put my hand to my mouth as we approached the lavish home.

"Are you okay?" he asked. "You don't look well. Are you going to have another one of your famous fainting spells?"

"I do feel a bit lightheaded," I admitted. "Probably just the stress from the situation. I'm not looking forward to going inside."

"Listen, darling, I won't leave your side. I swear. I'll be with you every step of the way. And if you land this deal, I'll bring you Starbucks every day for the next month."

"You always bring me Starbucks."

"Well, I'll throw in a couple of blueberry muffins, just to make you happy."

The mention of food made me think of my mother-in-law's comment. "Do I look like I've gained weight? And is my dress inappropriate? Helen acted like it was slutty."

"I think you look amazing, darling," Jacques said. "You might have gained a couple of pounds, but you've still got it going on."

"Thanks, I guess."

"When's Gregory coming home?"

"Hopefully later tonight."

He turned his head to wink at me. "My guess is that dress will wind up on the floor, then."

"Jacques!" I didn't want to elaborate but had a sneaking suspicion he was right. Although Greg always had been amorous, I was having a tough time keeping up with him in the romance department lately. And as much as I loved my husband, desire had been waning for me. I was pretty sure I was going through the change, and the thought depressed me to no end.

Jacques pulled his car into the enormous driveway lined with marble stone. A parking attendant helped us out of the car and gave Jacques a printed number on a card. He reached back into the vehicle to grab his briefcase and then stood, staring at the house. "It's even more spectacular close up."

Although it was early evening, the heat was still an oppressive ninety degrees, and I could feel a small puddle of sweat trickling down the center of my back. But my heart turned to ice as I looked up to gaze upon the home that had belonged to my dear departed friend.

Twenty-five years. Where had they gone to? I remembered the countless times I'd come here so that Paul and I could study, play movies on the VCR, or, once in a while, steal a bottle from the wine cellar. We'd had many heart-to-hearts and confided our dreams to one another. Paul had started working at the local hospital a few weeks before his death as a certified nursing assistant. He had planned to work there full-time for the entire summer before he left to attend college at Johns Hopkins in the fall. His dream had been to specialize in family medicine one day.

Despite the time lapse, it didn't seem as if much of the outside appearance had changed. The surrounding land, which I knew added up to about fifteen acres, was vibrant and green, with rose bushes and lilies in full bloom, despite the intense heat. My lawn was brown from the lack of rain we'd been having, and I imagined there must be landscapers who worked around the clock to keep the grounds of the estate looking fabulous. In addition to the terrace and in-ground pool behind the house, there was a small lake and nature trail that Paul and I had sometimes walked along.

Jacques grabbed the brass knocker of the heavy, polished oak door, and the sound echoed from the inside. He placed a protective hand on my arm. "Don't worry, girl. Everything will be fine."

We gave our names to the man who opened the front door. The entranceway opened into a large drawing room on the right that was empty at the moment. We followed him silently down a long, sterile hallway to the left, my heels clicking away on the travertine. Jacques' eyes darted back and forth as he took in every little detail. We passed the library with its inviting leather-bound books, the conservatory, billiard room, and a small sitting room where Paul and I would sometimes watch movies or study after school.

The butler opened the double doors of the dining room and addressed the room. "Mrs. Cindy York and her guest, Mr. Jacques Forte."

There were about fifty people in the room. Some were already seated at one of the two large, elegant tables that were adorned with china, crystal, and polished silver. Others milled about the large buffet table loaded down with lobster, shrimp, beef tenderloin tips in wine, various pasta dishes, and salads. A small bar had been set up in an opposite corner. A young man in a tuxedo was busy serving up wine and mixed drinks to a small crowd that was gathered in front.

A man with graying hair at the temples and light brown eyes that reminded me of Paul's stepped toward us. He grabbed my hand and gave me a small buss on the cheek. "Cindy. It's so good to see you. I knew you would come."

A lump formed in my throat and made speaking difficult. "It's nice to see you too, Ben."

"Cindy!" A woman squealed from behind Ben. Michelle Steadman hadn't aged much—if at all—since high school. The last time I'd seen her had been about nine or ten years ago at a nearby shopping mall. Her long, blonde hair was swept off her face and into a French twist. She wore a shimmering gold evening gown cut low in the front and even lower in the back. A slit ran up one side of the dress, revealing perfect, lithe legs, and a pair of matching four-inch stiletto heels I guessed were Jimmy Choos.

I stretched out my hand, but Michelle ignored it and grabbed me in a tight hug that surprised and almost smothered me.

"Michelle, you look terrific."

She smiled, displaying perfect white teeth suited for a Crest commercial. Not one wrinkle, gray hair, or anything out of place. I found myself wondering if she'd had work done. Okay, so I hoped.

"It's been way too long," she gushed. "The last time I saw you, you were pregnant with twins. My goodness, you'd been just about ready to pop!"

I smiled politely but didn't reply.

Jacques coughed lightly behind me.

"Oh, I'm sorry. This is my friend and boss, Jacques Forte from Forte Realty."

Ben reached past me to shake Jacques' hand. "It's wonderful to meet you. You're quite the giant in the real estate industry. I'm thrilled to know we'll be in such good hands."

Jacques puffed out his chest a bit. "The honor is ours, Mr. Steadman."

Ben placed his arm around Michelle's shoulders. "Why don't you two grab some dinner, and then we'll tour the house and talk privately."

"It will be a privilege to work for you and to find new owners for such a marvelous home," Jacques fawned. "Why, anyone would be happy here."

I winced inwardly at his statement but said nothing. I knew

Jacques didn't realize the effect his words might have upon me. A lavish home, personal chef, and hot sports cars did not a happy life make. Paul had been proof of that. It wasn't often that I disagreed with my best friend, but this was definitely one of those times.

No, Jacques. Not everyone had been happy here.

CHAPTER THREE

*J*acques and I found ourselves sitting across from
Melanie Flowers and Tonya Chase, two women I
remembered being a part of the so-called "greaser"
click in school. There'd been the preppies, smarties, nerds, and
the greasers, who'd frequented the smoking area of our school.
Paul had been part of the sophisticated preppies while I had
belonged to the elite "no one knows your name" group.

I remembered one occasion when Tonya had chased me
down the high school hall and threatened to beat me up because
she caught me staring at her boyfriend, Nick, during biology
class. I think the actual reason I'd been staring was because he'd
been picking his nose. Yeah, Nick was one who had definitely
been on my boyfriend wish list.

"I remember you," Tonya said in an accusatory voice. "What
kind of work do you do?"

I dipped a shrimp in cocktail sauce and prayed it wouldn't
wind up on my dress. "I'm a real estate agent. How about you?"

"Dog groomer." Tonya took a sip of her wine. She hadn't
changed much from high school—the same short, dark hair and

a skinny, almost borderline-anorexic build. Her teeth were yellow, probably from years of smoking. Various tattoos ran up and down her arms, and she had about fifty nose piercings. I tried hard not to stare, just in case she might leap out of her chair and chase me through the mansion.

Melanie nodded toward Jacques. With her dyed red hair in a bob, she looked like an older version of brat pack Molly Ringwald, only about fifty pounds heavier. "This your husband?"

"No," Jacques and I replied in unison.

"Jacques Forte." He nodded to them both. "Cindy works for me."

"Oh." Melanie winked at us. "*That's* how it is."

My face grew warm. "Um no, it isn't."

Melanie laughed. "I'm surprised to see you having an affair. You always seemed so square in high school."

I pursed my lips together tightly, afraid I might say something I'd regret. "You're way off base. I am *not* having an affair with Jacques."

"I'm gay," Jacques put in.

"Oh, please," Melanie said. "I can spot a gay guy a mile away. You definitely don't fit the bill."

"I can assure you, I'm gay," Jacques argued.

"Oh, have it your way." Melanie's expression was bored as she downed the rest of her beer.

I was afraid to look at Jacques in case there might be steam pouring out of his ears. I quickly changed the subject. "What do you do for a living, Melanie?"

"I'm a nurse at Burbank Hospital," she said in a matter of fact tone. "I work in the emergency room, but I used to be in maternity. I remember when you had your twins. How old are the little buggers now?"

"Eight," I said. "But I don't remember seeing you back then."

Melanie waved her hand in a dismissive manner. "I wasn't assigned to you, but trust me—I've always known everything that goes on in that hospital. I remember your old buddy Paul working there too, right before he offed himself."

The callous manner in which she referred to his suicide sickened me. For a moment, all I could do was stare in return. Finally, I found my voice and spoke with great care, enunciating every single word. "Don't ever talk about Paul like that."

She was taken aback by my tone. "Wow. It was twenty-five years ago, honey. Get over it already."

My eyes were growing moist. "I'm never going to be over it. He was my best friend and a wonderful person."

Melanie choked back a laugh. "Oh, please. Paul was a conceited snob. He walked around the hospital as if he owned the place. I was working there as a candy striper back then. We started at the same time, but he always acted like he was above me."

Jacques gave me a slight nudge, and I noticed that our conversation was starting to attract attention from others seated nearby. I couldn't have cared less.

"Besides," Tonya put in. "You couldn't have been that great of a friend if you didn't have any idea he was going to end it all."

I was so angry I couldn't see straight. Furious, I pushed my chair back and stood. "Excuse me. It's a bit stuffy in here, and I really need to get some air."

I walked out of the dining room into the hallway and found a marble-lined bathroom next to the kitchen. I studied my expression in the brass mirror over the sink. My hazel eyes had already started to fill. With a sigh, I brushed my forefinger across both eyelids. *Get it together. Time to confront the past.*

Instead of returning to the dining area, I ascended the winding, grand oak staircase. When I reached the first bedroom on the left side of the hall, I grabbed hold of the doorknob with both hands and turned. My entire body shook from head to toe as I entered the room.

My fears were unfounded. There wasn't one similarity that

linked the room to the one I remembered from so long ago. The bed, matching armoire, and posters of Bon Jovi and Nirvana that had adorned the walls were gone now. In their place was a roll-top desk, two velvet armchairs, and a gas fireplace. A small bookcase behind the desk held various binders and law books. I'd obviously stumbled upon Ben's private study.

I felt a hand on my shoulder and jumped about ten feet in the air. Ben stood behind me with a large cardboard box in his hand.

"Michelle and I redecorated after my parents' died. They'd been keeping his room a museum of sorts for years. We thought that wasn't healthy and decided it was time to make a fresh start."

I nodded without comment. It was ridiculous to think the room would be the same after all these years, but disappointment tugged at my heart strings. I was strangely possessive of Paul's personal space, and part of me was outraged that they'd dare disturb his things. I knew I was being irrational but couldn't help myself.

Ben patted the cardboard box. "Come on. I'm going to gather everyone in the drawing room for the main event."

Confused, I stared at the box. "What are you talking about?"

With a smile, he lifted a large steel tube out. Remnants of dirt clung to the outside. "Don't you remember what this is? My class had one too."

My jaw dropped as recognition set in. "Holy cow, it's our time capsule."

He smiled. "Your class buried it behind the school. Wasn't Mr. Remsen the English teacher?"

"History," I replied.

"Whatever. He was also your class advisor because Michelle received a phone call from him last week, reminding her about the capsule. She was excited when he offered to dig it up and bring the contents over today."

"How come Mr. Remsen's not here tonight? I would have loved to have seen him."

"He had plans of some sort, I guess. Anyhow, he asked us to take pictures and post them on Facebook so he could view them."

A chill swept over me as I stared at the tube. We'd buried that the day before Paul died. I found myself wondering if he'd already decided to take his life at that point. Why hadn't he talked to me about it first? Tonya was right. I should have had some clue. If I'd known, I would have tried to get him help or at least talk him out of it.

"Cindy, are you coming?"

Ben stood in the hallway, watching me with a puzzled expression. I cast one last look around the room and then followed him.

Jacques was waiting in the drawing room downstairs, his face pinched tight with worry. "There you are. I tried to catch up to you, but Michelle started asking me questions about the house. Everything okay?'

I smiled and linked my arm through his. "Just saying good-bye to some old ghosts."

He nodded in understanding as we followed Ben's tall figure back to the dining room. "I thought it was something like that. And don't pay any attention to nurse of the year in there. That chick has some serious issues, in my opinion."

Ben stood in the doorway but moved slightly to let us pass. Most of the crowd appeared to have finished eating, although some still milled around the buffet table, and I could have sworn I saw a woman stuffing shrimp into her purse.

Ben cleared his throat. "Attention, everyone. If you'll follow me into the drawing room, we have an event planned that I think you will all enjoy."

"But I haven't finished my lobster yet," Tonya protested with her mouth full.

"The food will remain out if anyone would like to come back for a second helping," Ben said. "And my waitstaff will be bringing out dessert trays soon. Please help yourselves."

Melanie raised her beer in mock salute. "The jerk does put on a good spread."

Jacques pressed his lips together tightly in an annoyed manner. "If you ladies detest the man so much, why in God's name did you bother to come?"

Melanie laughed. "I wouldn't have missed this for the world. No one puts on free high school reunions these days."

"It was very generous of Ben and Michelle to cover all the costs." I couldn't believe the gall of these women.

Tonya snorted. "Why shouldn't they? They have more money than God." She pushed back her chair and stood. Without another word to me or Jacques, she followed Melanie and the others out of the room.

Jacques watched their retreating figures in disgust. "The nerve of some people. Are you sure you're okay, love?"

I nodded. "I'm fine. Come on. The time capsule my class buried just before graduation is about to be opened, and I'm dying to see my contribution. Then we'll have a quick chat with Ben and Michelle about the house and hopefully take off."

"Sounds like a plan," Jacques agreed. "But I have to confess I'm not impressed with many of your *friends* here."

"For the record, they were never my friends. I had Paul, and that was about it. I didn't need anyone else."

He placed a comforting arm around my shoulders as we walked down the hall together. "Was there anything romantic brewing between the two of you?"

I laughed. "Not in the least." Then I hesitated. "Well, there was this one time—of course it didn't mean anything—"

"Oh, do tell," Jacques pleaded. We were standing in the back of the room, marveling at the Oriental rugs that covered the polished wood floors and the Queen Anne leather sofas and

wing chairs that were set up throughout the room. Ben placed
the box on a small antique table situated in the middle of the
room.

"It was just one of those crazy things. We snuck a bottle from
his parents' wine cellar. We were there alone and supposed to be
studying. For the first time in my life, I was certifiably drunk.
Then—Paul kissed me."

"And?" Jacques prodded.

"And that was all. Ben came home and found us, so I high-
tailed it out of there pretty fast."

Jacques arched his fine eyebrows. "What do you think would
have happened if Ben hadn't come home?"

I laughed again, but a weird sensation of heat spread
through my body as I remembered that night and how Paul had
been staring at me in a strange way. The next day, things
returned to normal, and we'd never mentioned that evening
again. Then, two weeks later, he'd picked up a gun and...

"Nothing," I assured him. "We were friends. That's all."

"Excuse me, Mr. Steadman." The elderly man who had
answered the door earlier approached Ben and waved his hand
in an attempt to get his attention. "Your client, Mr. Adelson, is
on the phone. He said it's urgent and can't wait."

Ben sighed and glanced around the room. "Thank you,
Wesley. Where did Mrs. Steadman wander off to?"

"I believe she's on a call herself. Miss Paula was in the room
with her," Wesley said.

"Who's Paula?" Jacques whispered.

"Their daughter," I replied. "She was named after Paul and
born a few months after he died."

Ben excused himself and started to walk past us, then
stopped. "Cindy, could you do the honors in my absence? I may
be a while. Would you mind passing out the envelopes to
everyone?"

"I'd be glad to." I approached the table with Jacques at my

side and stared down in wonder at the envelopes that had been
stuffed inside the capsule. I remembered how much fun it had
been filling out my sheet. Listing my best friend, what I wanted
to do after graduation, places I wanted to travel, etc. I couldn't
remember half of the answers now, but it would be a happy
diversion I looked forward to.

There had been two hundred people in our graduating class,
but only about sixty were present tonight. Not everyone had
chosen to fill out a sheet, but still, I was momentarily over-
whelmed by the pile of envelopes in front of me. I tried to sort
through them, matching them with the people I knew were
here, but the crowd was growing impatient already. I spotted
Melanie's right away and called her to retrieve it. She sauntered
over to us, a bored expression on her face.

"I have a sudden urge to smack her across the head," Jacques
whispered. "Do you think anyone would notice?"

"Yes, but they might not care," I murmured in response.

A few envelopes were left over as some classmates were not
here to receive them. People started looking at the responses
and were laughing to themselves and with other classmates.
Some chose to return to the dining room for dessert while
others made themselves at home on the sofas with espresso that
the butler served in demitasse cups.

I tore my envelope open while Jacques watched. He leaned
over my shoulder to read my written responses. "You wanted
six kids? Wow, you must have been high."

"Okay, if you're going to make fun of my answers, I'm won't
share them with you."

He chuckled and removed the paper from my hand despite
my protests. He read aloud in a halting manner. "Who will you
marry? Richard Gere? *Really?*"

"Oh, give me a break. I'd just seen *Pretty Woman.*"

He clucked his tongue in disdain as he read further. "What I want to do after graduation. Go to Hollywood and become an actress." He laughed so hard I feared he might hurt himself. Or maybe I secretly hoped he would.

I snatched the paper away from him and stuffed it into my dress pocket. "That does it. You've had enough of a laugh at my expense."

"Now listen Cin, I—"

I glanced down at the remaining envelopes and started to stuff them back into the capsule. One had stuck to the back of another, and as I separated them, my body froze. I raised the envelope in my trembling hand.

"What's wrong?"

I raised the envelope higher so that he could see the name *Paul Steadman* written in large, block letters on the front.

Jacques flinched. "Oh boy."

My mouth resembled sawdust as I struggled to speak. "We buried these the day before—he... I wasn't with him when he brought his over. I didn't know he... He said it was silly." I knew I wasn't making any sense but couldn't stop myself from rambling.

Jacques took my hand in his. "Come on, dear. We'll go read this in private."

"I don't know." I followed him down the hall while tightly clutching the envelope in my hand. "Shouldn't Ben be the one to open it?"

"If he asks, I'll say it's my fault. That I opened it by mistake. Go ahead, dear. Maybe it will give you some kind of peace. Lord knows you need some. Perhaps the note will help you to understand why he did what he did."

That's what I hoped for, or rather, was afraid of.

We entered the billiard room. Jacques shut the door behind us, and I turned the envelope over. Beads of sweat gathered on my forehead. "I want to see what's in it, but I'm scared, Jacques."

Jacques nodded, a somber expression on his face. "Do you want me to read it first?"

I shook my head. "No, I should do it."

I slid my fingernail along the edge of the flap and opened it. To my surprise, there was another envelope inside, with my name printed on it.

My blood ran cold. "Oh my God. He wrote this to me." Could I deal with a personalized suicide note now? I didn't think so.

I struggled to breathe normally as I opened the second envelope and found the designated sheet classmates had been given. Instead of filing out the responses, Paul had written, "See Other Side" across the page. I turned it over to find his handwritten note.

Hey Cin,

You know I'm not much for these things. I wasn't even going to do this but thought it might be fun to leave a message for you instead. I can hardly wait to see your face when you open this in 25 years. Hopefully I'll be standing beside you.

I guess you must know by now how I feel about you. That kiss two weeks ago was no accident. I've loved you since the second grade but never had the courage to tell you before. There're only two things I want out of life—to be the best damn doctor I can and spend the rest of my time with you.

I've already decided tomorrow is when I'll tell you the truth, when we get together to study. If you don't feel the same, well, at least I tried. But I'm so confident it won't affect our friendship that I'm sure we can laugh about it someday. I think you feel the same way about me, but maybe you just don't know it yet. Tomorrow I will find out, and nothing will stop me from telling you.

I love you,

Paul

I was aware of Jacques' gasp as he read the letter over my shoulder. I continued to stare at the page, unable to move.

"Are you all right?"

The paper slowly fluttered through the air, and the blood roared in my ears. Words failed me, and my legs resembled heavy blocks of cement. I turned to Jacques, his face blurred by my tears. I felt myself starting to fall and reached out my hand to him. He was quick to grab me before my body hit the floor.

I blinked and saw Jacques' worried face come into focus above mine. I was lying on the floor of the billiard room. Jacques was on his knees beside me, his arm behind the back of my head, supporting it.

"Thank God," he breathed. "I was just about to call 9-1-1. Are you okay, love?"

I nodded and tried to sit up, but Jacques' firm grip held me in place.

"No. You stay here and rest for a few minutes. I'm going to find the butler and ask him to bring you some tea."

"I can't believe it," I whispered.

He patted my cheek. "It had to be quite a shock for you to read about his feelings for you after all this time. You never had any idea?"

I shook my head. "None. But that's not what I…I'm talking about." I shut my eyes tight as a bout of nausea swept over me. I tried to blink away tears but knew they'd continue to fall anyway.

When I opened my eyes again, Jacques' confused gaze met mine. "You're not making any sense."

"I have my answer, after all these years."

Recognition slowly dawned on my best friend's face. "You mean you know why he killed himself?"

Despite Jacques' protests, I forced myself into an upright position. He remained sitting beside me on the floor, patiently waiting for me to answer his question.

I took several deep, cleansing breaths and clasped his hand

tightly between mine. "No. It all makes perfect sense now. And I was stupid for not realizing this years ago."

"Okay, love, now you're really confusing me. Out with it."

I flicked my eyes toward his face. "Paul didn't commit suicide, Jacques. He was murdered."

CHAPTER FOUR

he room was silent, except for the ticking sound emanating from the impressive oak grandfather clock. Jacques and I remained sitting on the floor, and he had one hand on the small of my back as he continued to support me. I was vaguely aware of laughter coming from down the hall. I started to shiver, and Jacques quickly removed his suit coat and placed it around my shoulders.

"How can you be so sure?"

I waved the letter in the air. "This is more than enough proof for me. He never would have written something like this if he was going to kill himself. Now I understand why his suicide never made sense to me."

"Did you love him too?"

I hesitated for a moment. I hadn't been expecting that question and tried to collect my thoughts. "I—I don't know. In my own way, I guess."

Jacques face was sympathetic. "What would you have done if he'd spilled his guts to you the next day?"

We winced simultaneously. "Ouch. Damn. Bad choice of words. I'm sorry, Cin. That came out wrong."

I shut my eyes, seeing the blood splattered on the bed once again and Paul's lifeless body in a fetal position. I remembered how I'd rushed over and felt for his pulse. There had been a very faint one, but even though the EMT had arrived quickly after my call, he'd been pronounced dead shortly after arriving at the hospital.

"Are you going to faint again?"

I shook my head and, with Jacques' assistance, slowly rose to my feet. I clutched his jacket around me for warmth. In short, I felt awful. My head was spinning, and my stomach was grumbling in a manner that did not depict hunger. "I don't think I'll be able to discuss the details of the house tonight. Would you mind if we rescheduled with Ben? Maybe for tomorrow?"

He smiled sympathetically. "Of course. Let me go and see if I can find him before we leave, and I'll explain everything. You wait here."

I clutched his arm. "Let me tell him about the letter, please."

"Whatever you say, darling. Don't move. I shall return."

I grabbed the side of the pool table for support. Yes, it all made sense to me now. Why hadn't I figured this out years ago? I was convinced this was the reason I'd had the recurring nightmares and never made peace with the situation. Deep down, I knew Paul would never do something like that.

Nothing will stop me from telling you tomorrow.

Those were not the words of someone who planned to commit suicide. Those were the words of someone determined, who knew his own mind, and went after what he wanted. I should have trusted my friend more.

What would I have said if he'd confessed his love to me? I would have been shocked, but would I have given him a chance? We'd gone to the prom the week before but only as friends. I'd loved everything about Paul but never thought about him in a romantic way. And for years, he'd been in love with me. He could have had any girl he wanted, but instead he'd been in love with shoestring Cindy. *Me.*

Before I could analyze the situation any further, Jacques returned with Ben. He opened his mouth in shock as he took in my appearance. "Cindy, you look awful. Jacques said you'd like to postpone the tour and contract signing because you're not feeling well. Are you sure you're okay? Can I bring you anything?"

I shook my head. "No, thank you. It'll pass. We'd like to come by tomorrow, if that's okay with you and Michelle."

"Since it's Sunday, that will work out well for us. How about one o'clock? You could both come for brunch."

The mention of food wasn't sitting well with my stomach. "That sounds great, thank you."

"I left a copy of the contract on your desk and some comps to browse," Jacques said to Ben. "This way you can look it over ahead of time, and let us know if you have questions."

"Perfect," Ben said. He escorted us down the hall to the front door while Jacques handed me my purse that he'd retrieved from the drawing room.

Ben leaned over and bussed me on the cheek. "I know how difficult this must have been for you. Not a day goes by that I don't think about him too."

My breath caught in my throat. "Ben, I—"

Jacques shook his head at me. "Tomorrow, dear. You two can discuss everything then."

We were silent on the drive back to my house, and I looked at my watch. It wasn't even ten o'clock yet. When Jacques pulled into my driveway, I glanced around, hopeful, but only my car and my mother-in-law's Chevy were visible.

I sighed. "I need Greg."

He squeezed my hand. "I'm sure he'll be home as soon as he can, darling."

I pinched the bridge of my nose between my thumb and

forefinger. "What am I going to say to Ben and Michelle tomorrow? They're going to think I'm nuts."

He grinned wickedly. "Just let them sign the contract first, okay?"

"Oh, you!" I smiled but then grew serious again. "I can't let this go. Deep down I've always known something didn't make sense. I need to find out who did this to Paul."

Jacques gave me a grim look. "It's been twenty-five years. Where on earth would you even start?"

I blew out a long breath. "I don't know. Maybe we could find the police officer who came to the house that day. I'll do whatever I have to."

"Well, count me in."

"Jacques, this is my problem."

"You're my best friend, and I love you. I understand how much this must have tormented you all these years. Plus, we do make a great team, remember?"

I smiled. "Poirot and Hastings to the rescue." When Jacques and I had worked together at Hospitable Homes, a coworker had been murdered, and a great deal of suspicion had been thrown on me when I'd been the one to discover her body. With Jacques' help, I'd managed to clear my name and find the real killer, but we'd both almost lost our lives during the process. "You've got a deal. What would I do without you?"

Jacques turned his nose up in the air. "Let's hope you never have to find out, darling." He stepped out of the vehicle and went around to open my door. Then he kissed my cheek and hugged me. "Get some sleep. No hanky-panky with Gregory tonight. I'll pick you up around twelve-thirty."

I grinned. "See you tomorrow. And thanks."

He got behind the wheel, blew me a kiss, and zoomed off.

I unlocked the front door quietly and took my shoes off in the small foyer. I padded through the living room and into the kitchen, positive I'd find my mother-in-law removing items from my fridge and cleaning it. No such luck. I glanced into the study. No Helen there either. Maybe she was upstairs reading the boys a bedtime story, although they were hopefully asleep by now.

I ascended the stairs in my bare feet. I passed my bedroom and caught sight of Helen out of the corner of my eye. I pushed the door open all the way, and she jumped. She was rummaging through the top drawer of my nightstand. The composure I'd been struggling for all evening flew out the window.

"What are you doing in here?" I snapped.

My mother-in-law's face went crimson. "I, uh, was folding some of your laundry and putting it away for you."

What a crock. "Don't give me that. You were snooping around in my things."

She gave a small laugh. "I would never do something like that. You are way out of line, Cynthia."

"I'd say *you're* the one out of line. Thanks for watching the boys, and have a safe drive home." I almost said have a safe ride home on your broom, but stopped myself just in time.

She tossed her head defiantly at me. "Well, that's gratitude. My poor son. I did try to warn him, all those years ago. He could have done so much better."

I pressed my lips together tightly. Most of the time I tried to avoid confrontations with Helen, but tonight my patience was wearing thin. "I know you're going to hate hearing this, but your son happens to love me and always will. Perhaps you should find a way to deal with it."

Helen narrowed her eyes but chose to ignore my remark. "I'll see myself out." Without another word, she flounced past me and hurried down the staircase. I followed at a respectable distance while she rushed into the kitchen to retrieve her purse and tote bag. She headed for the front door, almost colliding with Darcy, who had just walked in.

"Sorry, Grandma."

"Good night, darling." Helen said to Darcy and then cut her eyes to me angrily.

"Come back when you can stay longer," I called. *Not.*

Darcy stared at me, puzzled. She was a beautiful girl with shoulder-length, black hair and enormous dark eyes. I put an arm around her and steered her into the kitchen.

"What was all that about?" she asked.

I waved my hand impatiently. "Just your grandmother being your grandmother. Never mind her. How was the concert?"

She made a face. "Awful. The lawn was so packed we couldn't even see them. Plus, it was hotter than hell out there."

"Darcy!"

"Sorry." She watched as I pulled a bottle of wine out of the fridge. "You hardly ever drink."

"Well, I really need one tonight because of your grandmother." And thanks to the news I'd learned earlier.

Darcy turned on the faucet and helped herself to a glass of water. "Is Daddy coming home tonight?"

I reached for a wine glass in the cupboard and filled it to capacity. "He's supposed to."

"You miss him, don't you?"

I patted her cheek. "I always miss him when he goes away. Do you want something to eat?"

She shook her head. "I'm not hungry. Um, do you think we could talk for a minute?"

"Of course, honey. Come on—let's go into the living room."

She followed me, and we both plopped ourselves down onto the couch. Rusty entered the room and settled himself at our feet.

I took a long sip of my drink and then tucked my feet underneath me. "What's up?"

She stared down at the floor. "Varsity cheerleading tryouts start next week."

"I remember. We're going to carpool with Heather's mom, right?"

She bit into her lower lip. "I'm really scared I won't make it. There're a lot of girls trying out this year."

"Could you stay on junior varsity for another year?"

Darcy gazed at me with a determined glint in her eyes. "I'd rather die first. But there's a new coach for varsity this year. Everyone's saying that she's already picked out some of the girls she wants for the squad."

I opened my mouth in surprise. "Well, that isn't fair. Maybe I should talk to the principal."

"No!" Darcy begged. "That would make things worse. Please, Mom. I just was wondering if maybe I could work with a private trainer a few times. I could help pay for it with the babysitting money I've earned. I—"

"Darcy, slow down. I don't know if we can afford—" I stopped myself and stared into her mournful face, then sighed. At that moment, a light bulb clicked on inside my head. "Wait a second. I met someone tonight who used to be a choreographer for the Jets cheerleaders. Maybe she'd be willing to help."

Darcy's jaw almost hit the floor. "Oh my God. Are you totally serious?"

I grinned. "Well, I'd have to check with her first, so don't get your hopes up. But I'll see her tomorrow and promise to do what I can."

"Oh, Mommy, I love you!" She squealed and threw her arms around my neck.

"Okay, you'd better get to bed. We'll talk about it in the morning."

Darcy kissed me on the cheek and hugged me again. "Night. You're the best mother ever."

I watched her slender figure run up the carpeted staircase and smiled to myself. Today I was the world's best mom.

Tomorrow could be a different story. Might as well enjoy it while it lasted.

I settled back on the couch with my wine and took another sip. My mind was already racing with things to say to Ben and Michelle tomorrow. It would be easier to do this with their support, but no matter what, I'd already decided to conduct my own investigation and wouldn't let them dissuade me.

Headlights shone through the front window, and I pulled the curtain back. Rusty barked and rushed to the front door. I watched as Greg stepped out of the vehicle and locked it with his remote. I hurried to the door and pulled it open for him. He dropped his overnight bag and lifted me off my feet and into his arms.

"God, I missed you," I breathed.

Greg chuckled as he kissed me. "Mm, this is a nice welcome. Maybe I should go away more often."

"Do me a favor and don't." I ran my fingers through his curly, light brown hair, which was slightly disheveled, as usual.

Greg's bright blue eyes regarded me sharply. He shut the door behind him and stooped down to pet Rusty. "Something's wrong, baby. What is it?"

"Old ghosts," I said.

He stared, puzzled, and then put his arm around me as we settled back on the couch. "What are you talking about? Are the kids okay?"

I assured him they were fine and as quickly as I could, explained what had transpired earlier at the mansion. Greg listened patiently, his expression sober. His reaction was similar to Jacques.

"Cin, this happened twenty-five years ago. Where on earth would you start?"

"I'm going to ask Ben if he has any information to share with me," I said. "Then I'll see if I can find out who the lead investigator was on the case."

"It's a small town," Greg said. "There probably wasn't even a lead investigator back then. The police department may have handled it on their own, especially if they ruled Paul's case a suicide from the beginning."

It would have been easy to give up at that point, but I knew I couldn't. "I have to try, Greg. I need to know."

His eyes searched mine. "This note he left you. What exactly did it say?"

Oh, boy. "H-he told me he was in love with me."

Greg was silent for a few seconds as he digested this. "What about you? Were you in love with him?"

I thought I caught a hint of jealousy in my husband's tone, which was ridiculous since I hadn't even known him back then. I tried to be completely honest. "We never had that kind of relationship. I loved him as a friend, a brother. I don't know what I would have done if he'd had the chance to tell me about his feelings. I do know I wouldn't have let it ruin our friendship though."

He reached down to pet Rusty again, not saying anything.

I had to ask. "Does this bother you?"

Greg smiled, and I snuggled up against his massive chest. "No. Why would it bother me? The guy obviously had good taste. I didn't even know you back then. I guess for a split second I found myself wondering what might have happened if he'd lived. Maybe you two would have gotten married instead."

A scenario I'd never thought about before. "That's doubtful. Like I said, I didn't have those types of feelings for him."

"But if he'd admitted his love to you like he'd planned, that could have changed everything. It might have divulged feelings you never even knew you were capable of."

It was obvious Greg was trying to analyze the entire situation, something he didn't usually bother with. "I don't think so. I was meant to be with you."

He gazed into my eyes and covered my mouth with his. "Just

be careful, baby. I know this is important to you, but if your theory is correct, someone has gotten away with murder for a long time. And they're not going to like you poking around."

"I'll be fine. I promise."

He kissed me again then nuzzled my neck. "I think we should go upstairs and celebrate my homecoming. What do you say?"

I was grateful he couldn't see my face at that moment. As much as I loved Greg, I had no desire for celebrating. And this was odd since I always enjoyed being with my husband. *What the heck was wrong with me lately?*

Greg moved his head back so that he could study my face. His expression was wounded. "You don't want to?"

The last thing I wanted to do was hurt his feelings. "I do want to. It's just—well, I think there's something going on with me."

"Yeah, I've noticed. You don't seem to be interested lately."

I winced. "God, I hate saying this, but I think I'm going through the change, and it's affecting—everything, if you know what I mean."

"Maybe you should go to the doctor and get some hormones."

I didn't know whether to laugh or cry. "And then what? Grow hair on my chin? Gain thirty pounds?"

He grinned. "I'd love you even if you had a mustache."

"This isn't funny, Greg. I'm getting old."

He kissed my neck and unzipped my dress down the back. "No, you're not. You're getting better. Come on. I'll prove it to you."

With a sigh, I got up from the couch and followed him to the stairs. He kissed me again, and a faint stirring somewhere reassured me that perhaps not all of my female parts were dead.

We reached the door of our bedroom. Greg opened it and then stepped back to allow me to enter first. He scooped up our cat, Sweetie, from the bed, and placed her out in the hallway, despite her meows of protest. "Yeah, I know. Everyone has an attitude around here."

Greg shut and locked the door, then turned around with that teasing grin on his face that I loved and knew all too well.

He pulled me into his arms. "This is all your fault for making me—"

I interrupted, thinking of the episode with the twins' earlier. "You're not going to say the *H* word, are you?"

His expression was puzzled. "Happy?"

"THAT WORKS TOO."

CHAPTER FIVE

*T*he bright sunshine streaming through my bedroom window woke me. I glanced at the alarm clock on my nightstand. Ten-thirty. Holy cow. I never slept this late. I grabbed my robe from the bottom of the bed and was just about to run downstairs when Greg appeared in the doorway with a tray in his hand.

"You shouldn't have let me sleep this late," I chided. "I've got to get the kids breakfast. And Jacques will be here to pick me up at twelve-thirty."

He gestured toward the bed. "I've already fed the kids. Get back in bed, and enjoy your breakfast. That's an order, my darling."

I was both touched and pleased. "Yes, sir."

Greg placed the tray on my knees. There were fresh strawberries, eggs, toast, juice, and coffee. I stared at him, astonished. "When did you have time to do all this?"

He stretched out lazily next to me on the bed and handed me a napkin. "I've been up since six."

My mouth fell open. "Did you even sleep?"

Greg grinned as he put his arms around me and kissed me.

"Who needs sleep? I feel great. Completely energized."

What the heck? Greg had driven over three hours the night before and by my calculations, had about four hours of sleep at the most. So how did he have energy when I had zero?

"I'm going through a middle-age crisis while you're aging in reverse."

He roared with laughter. "You look tired, baby. I mean, you're still gorgeous and all, but you do look kind of wiped out. Guess that's my fault, huh?"

"I believe you did have a hand in it, yes."

He grinned and removed the tray from my knees, placing it on the nightstand. "Speaking of which, I'd love to spend some more time with my beautiful wife right now." He wrapped his arms around me again while I struggled to free myself.

"Jeez Louise. What are you, Superman?" I asked.

The smile faded from his face. "Is something else going on that you're not telling me? You just don't seem yourself lately."

"I told you, it's the change. Things will get better." At least I hoped so.

"Call your doctor tomorrow, and make an appointment," he said. "How long has it been since you've had a physical?"

I got to my feet and walked over to the closet to find a skirt and blouse for my meeting with Ben and Michelle. "Um—five years? Maybe more?"

He came up behind me and put his arms around my waist. "That's way too long. And if it is what you say, maybe the doctor can prescribe something to make you feel better." He kissed my ear while I tried not to giggle.

"Okay, you *have* to stop. I need to jump in the shower."

He turned me around and kissed me passionately. "I could jump in with you."

"No!"

Greg smiled as he released me and then picked up the tray from the nightstand. He stood at the bedroom door, with one hand on the knob. "I'll leave you alone as long as I can have a rain check tonight."

He winked and shut the door.

Sheesh. I supposed I should be thrilled that after eighteen years of marriage my husband still found me attractive. But all I wanted to do was sleep. Twenty-four hours a day. And he was acting like he could run the Boston Marathon. How was this even fair?

I showered and dressed, feeling much better afterward. I went downstairs to do the breakfast dishes. Greg was out back playing touch football with the boys while Darcy was upstairs in her room on the phone. I grabbed another cup of coffee while I waited for Jacques and thought back to what Greg had said about calling my doctor.

I hadn't seen my primary physician, Dr. Sanchez, in about seven or eight years. The last two times I'd scheduled a physical he'd been on vacation, so I'd gone to another doctor in his office instead. I was hoping he'd be available since I knew he'd worked briefly with Paul that one summer. Maybe he'd remember something that could assist me in my investigation. It was a long shot, but I didn't know where else to start right now.

I grabbed a notepad from the kitchen drawer and began to make a list of people who might be able to shed some light on the incident. I started with Ben, then the police department. Perhaps talking to some other classmates could prove useful as well. How I wish I'd done this years ago. Were Jacques and Greg right? Could I discover anything to back my theory about Paul after all these years?

I owed it to my friend to at least try.

"ARE YOU FEELING BETTER, CINDY?" Michelle asked as she poured coffee from a silver teapot on her back terrace. "Ben said you didn't look well last night. I hope it wasn't something you ate here."

I shook my head. "Not at all. And I'm fine, thank you."

Jacques and Ben were doing a walk-through of the house. Jacques had insisted I stay put, and for once, I hadn't argued with him. Besides, I knew the place like the back of my hand. The mansion was almost 7,000 square feet, so I was happy to sit on the terrace and rest, despite the oppressive heat.

I hesitated for a moment. "I was wondering if I could ask you a favor."

"Of course. Anything for an old high school chum."

I blinked. Michelle had never given me the time of day in high school. I hated to ask for favors, but when it came to my children, their happiness was my priority. "I know you have a great deal of experience with cheerleading and choreography."

She sipped her drink. "I don't work for the Jets anymore, but I'd be happy to ask promotions about tickets for a game for you. I still have connections. How many do you need?"

I laughed. "That's not what I was after, thanks. My daughter, Darcy, is trying out for the varsity cheerleading squad at her high school this year. She'd love some pointers. If you have time, of course."

Her eyes gleamed. "Why, I'd love to! Is it Burbank High?"

I blew out a sigh of relief. "Yes, our alma mater. And thank you. She's so worried about making the team this year. I guess there's a lot of competition."

Michelle nodded soberly. "Those girls work so hard. And they don't get near the respect they deserve. Some of them even work harder than the football players. It's not all about looks, like people think."

I smiled but didn't reply. That was exactly what I'd thought of Michelle back then.

Michelle picked up her phone and scrolled the screen. "Let's see. I have some free time this Tuesday afternoon. Why don't I meet her over at the football field for the Valley Dogs? Ben and I are corporate sponsors, and they allow us to use the facilities whenever we like. How about four o'clock? I believe they finish their practices around two."

I smiled. "She'll be there. It's wonderful of you to do this. Darcy will be absolutely thrilled."

She waved her hand dismissively. "Oh, please. I'll enjoy it too. I miss the sport so much."

"Excuse me. I just wanted to say good-bye, Mom."

I glanced up to see a striking young blonde woman standing by the French doors with a small suitcase in her hand.

Michelle rose to her feet as the young woman crossed over to the chrome-and-glass table where we were seated. She kissed her on the cheek and then beamed at me. "Cindy, this is our daughter, Paula. I wasn't sure if you'd ever met her."

I stood to shake Paula's hand. She was almost an exact replica of her mother only taller, with the same emerald eyes, a tiny nose, and fine hair so blonde it was almost white.

Paula smiled politely at me. "It's very nice to meet you. I believe mom said you were the real estate agent?"

I nodded. "That's right."

"Well, I know that mom is anxious for dad to retire so they can enjoy their condo in Bermuda," Paula said. "I hope you're able to sell the house quickly."

"I'll do everything I can to make your parents happy."

Michelle flashed a perfect smile. "We have no doubt about that."

"Will you be moving with your parents?" I asked.

Paula shook her head. "I'll visit, of course, but I have my own life in New York City. I'm a massage therapist there. I love the glamour and the craziness of the big city. Bermuda's too tame by my standards."

"Ah, sweetheart." Ben appeared in the doorway with Jacques next to him. "I was afraid I might have missed you."

She walked over to her father and hugged him tightly. "I never would have left without saying good-bye, Daddy. You know that." She smiled at Jacques as a horn sounded from out front. "That's my ride. I'll see you in a couple of weeks."

"Do be careful, darling." Michelle blew her daughter a kiss.

When she had departed, Jacques and Ben seated themselves at the table. Michelle offered Jacques coffee, but he refused.

Michelle watched her husband. "So what's the verdict?"

Ben waved the contract. "It's official. Jacques said the sign will go up tomorrow morning."

"Marvelous." Michelle sipped her mimosa. "The sooner we can leave this state, the better. I really don't understand my daughter's zest for city life. I can barely tolerate it here, and our estate is private. Plus, I detest the cold weather."

I smiled. "I can certainly understand that. Although it is a little hard to imagine on a day like today." That was an under-statement. There was a light breeze, but the heat was still oppressive, and I could feel another headache coming on.

Michelle laughed. "Oh, I love this type of weather. The hotter, the better." She drained her glass and reached for the pitcher to refill it. "Would you like one, Jacques?"

"No, thank you," Jacques murmured.

Ben cleared his throat. "There is one thing I'd like to ask about the sale of the house."

"Of course. Anything," Jacques said.

Ben looked directly at me. "Is it necessary to divulge what happened to Paul here? I mean, I know that there are people in town who remember, of course, but say we get an out-of-town buyer, which Jacques told me might be the case. Do they have to be told in advance?"

"No," I answered. "We are not required to tell potential buyers that someone died here. Of course, if a client were to ask me directly, I hope you understand that I would feel oblig-ated to give them an honest response. But in answer to your question, New York agents do not have to disclose it on the listing."

Jacques caught my eye and winked in approval.

Ben nodded. "Good to hear. People are funny about things like that sometimes, you know?"

We were all silent for a moment, while I watched Jacques' face. He knew what I was about to say next and nodded slightly, as if encouraging me to proceed.

I took a sip of my ice water. "There's something I'd like to discuss with both of you, and I'm afraid it's going to come as a bit of a shock."

Ben and Michelle exchanged confused glances.

"Of course, Cindy," Ben said. "Please continue."

I swallowed nervously. "Last night, at the reunion, there was an envelope from Paul in the time capsule. I went ahead and opened it. I'm sorry, I should have checked with you first."

Ben smiled. "That's all right. But I would like to see it. As you know, we never found a suicide note, so this may have been the last letter he ever wrote."

"Yes," Michelle said. "I'd love to see it too."

Doubtful, I reached into my purse. "It actually was a note to me."

Ben extended his hand forward. "I would still like to see it."

Ugh. "This is a bit embarrassing for me," I confessed. "It has nothing to do with his suicide, I assure you. Actually, it's quite the opposite. It's a love letter to me—of sorts."

Ben's mouth fell open in surprise. "I had no idea you two were involved in a romantic manner back then. But it does make sense."

Heat warmed my face to the point I thought I might suffocate from embarrassment. "No. You misunderstand me. We were friends. That's all. He was confiding his true feelings to me for the first time."

"How beautiful." Michelle studied my face. "So, did you refuse him? Is that why he—"

I shook my head vigorously. "*No.* It wasn't like that."

"Cindy, dear," Jacques said quietly. "Just let them see the letter."

With a sigh, I passed the envelope to Ben. He removed the sheet and read silently as Michelle leaned over his shoulder. When they finished, they exchanged a glance, and then their gazes came to rest on me.

"Wow," Ben said. "That's quite an admission. I had no idea. I though he was involved with that other girl. You remember, Michelle. She was a cheerleader with you. Long blonde hair, big mouth, equally big chest."

Michelle glared at her husband. "Really, Ben. Is that all you men ever see?"

Jacques bent his head slightly so no one could see the smile forming at the corners of his mouth.

"Rachel Kennedy," Michelle said. "I know she had the hots for Paul back then. Everyone knew it. But apparently he didn't reciprocate her feelings." She arched one well-groomed eyebrow at me.

My face was hot underneath my fingertips. "I had no idea of Paul's true feelings."

"So, he didn't kill himself because you rejected him?" Ben asked.

They clearly weren't getting it. I struggled to maintain my composure. "*No.* But there is something more to this. Don't you see?"

They both shrugged. "Please explain," Ben said.

Out with it. "I'm convinced Paul didn't commit suicide. I believe he was murdered."

Michelle gasped and covered her mouth with her hands. Ben remained frozen in his chair, his eyes transfixed on me. Jacques reached for my hand and squeezed it in encouragement. I waited for Ben to start screaming, tear up the contract, or ask us to leave the premises.

He didn't do any of those things. Instead, he shifted his weight and grasped the arms of his chair. "I think you're right."

"You do?" Michelle and I both said simultaneously.

Ben nodded. "It never seemed to fit. I mean, he just wasn't the sort. He'd been acting a bit strange that morning, I'll grant you. Said he needed to talk to me about something, but I told him I didn't have the time." He lowered his head and stared into his lap. "I never told anyone this. But maybe if I'd made time for him, things could have been different. Your theory—it fits."

I breathed a sigh of relief. "Thank goodness. I was afraid you might think I was crazy."

"Not at all." He stared at Michelle, who smiled and rubbed her palm against the back of his head affectionately. "Perhaps I always knew but didn't want to face the truth."

I nodded. "That's how I feel too. The problem is, where do we go from here?"

We were all silent for a moment.

"Cindy, this happened so long ago," Ben said. "Any clues to prove your theory are probably long gone."

"That's not good enough for me," I replied. "He was my best friend, and I loved him like a brother too. For what it's worth, I'm going to do my damnedest to make sure someone pays for this."

Michelle's green eyes grew large and round. "Where would you even start?"

"Do you remember who might have been in charge of the inquiry?" I asked Ben. "Did they call in an investigator? Was an autopsy performed on Paul?"

Ben shook his head. "I can't be positive, but I don't think there was an autopsy. Mom and Dad were pretty messed up afterward. I remember her crying that she didn't want anyone taking him apart."

I winced at the thought. "Your parents were never the same after his death." In my mind at least, Paul's death had led to the early demise of their mother. She'd passed away from a stroke a year after his death, at the young age of forty-six. Only a couple of years older than I was now. It was unnerving.

I'd been present at Mrs. Steadman's funeral, but when Paul's father died, I'd just given birth to Darcy and been unable to attend, so I'd sent a card with my regrets. "Do you remember the name of any of the policemen involved?"

Ben took a sip from his water glass. "The lead detective was named Connors. Aaron Connors. He retired a few years ago. The only reason I even remember is because I handled divorce proceedings for his wife."

Jacques made a face. "With all due respect, he may not be thrilled about hearing the Steadman name again."

Ben laughed. "It wasn't like that. Both were in complete agreement about the divorce."

I leaned forward. "Would you have an address for him?"

"Not on hand," Ben replied. "But I'll ask my secretary to find it, and I'll send you a text in the morning with his information."

"That would be great. Thanks," I said.

His voice was almost wistful as he stared at me. "I wish you the best of luck, Cindy. And if there's anything Michelle and I can do to help, please let us know."

CHAPTER SIX

*E*verything was perfect. The hot sun was beating down on my body as Greg and I relaxed in chaise lounges by the turquoise colored water in Bermuda. There was no one around for miles. He leaned over and kissed my ear.

I giggled. "Stop it. I'm too tired."

The kissing became more intense, and he ended up biting my ear. "Ouch! Don't do that!"

Shrieks of laughter pierced my dream. I opened one eye, glanced over my shoulder, and saw Rusty sitting next to me in bed, his tongue working its way across my face.

I pushed the dog away. "Ew, stop!"

The twins were standing in the doorway, laughing so hard I thought they might double over in pain for a split second.

I rubbed my eyes wearily and sat up. "What time is it?"

"Eight o'clock," Seth replied. He jumped on the bed and hugged Rusty to him. "Were you dreaming about Dad, Mom?"

I flung back the covers and reached for my robe at the bottom of the bed. "More or less. Speaking of your father, where is he?"

"Downstairs having coffee," Stevie said. "I think he's leaving

for work soon. He gave us cereal and toast when he came back
from his jog."

That stopped me in my tracks. I turned around to look at the
twins, who were both on my bed now with the dog. "Your father
went *jogging*?"

"Yeah." Stevie reached for the television remote on my nightstand. "Then he said he needed a cold shower."

Oh boy.

I left the twins tussling on my bed and padded my way down
the stairs in search of coffee. Greg was sitting at the kitchen
table, reading the newspaper.

"Good morning," I said.

He reached out and grabbed me, pulling me onto his lap.
"Morning, beautiful."

"You should have woken me earlier."

"You looked so pretty while you were sleeping, I just couldn't
bring myself to do it." He pushed my hair back and frowned.
"Why is your ear all wet?"

"It was Rusty's turn to show me some love this morning."

Greg grinned and then placed his lips over mine. "Hmm.
Let's go away next weekend. I'll make us a reservation at some
out-of-the-way hotel by the beach."

I sighed and removed his arm so that I could stand. "Honey,
we shouldn't spend the money right now. And this heat is
killing me. I really don't feel like doing anything."

He stared at me over the rim of his coffee mug. "Are you still
feeling sick?"

I didn't want to worry him. "I'm just tired. It will pass."

Greg was silent as he continued to watch me. I picked my
cell phone off the counter where I'd left it the night before and
scrolled through my messages. Three voicemails. A text from
Ben Steadman had arrived with Aaron Connors's home phone
number, and there was a text from Jacques as well. *Client wants
to see the Steadman mansion tomorrow! Score one for us!*

"Cin, I think this whole episode with Paul is upsetting you more than you realize. And now that you're selling a house for his brother—well, I don't know if that's a good thing."

I turned around to face him. "You might be right. I've felt so crappy since this whole thing started. But I'd feel even worse if I didn't do anything."

He came over and put his arms around me. "Promise me you'll call your doctor today?"

I nodded. "I will. But I'm dreading the visit. No woman actually wants to hear that she's going through menopause."

Greg wove his fingers through my hair. "It makes no difference. You'll always be beautiful to me."

"How come men don't go through a change?"

He grinned as he kissed me. "We're like fine wine. We just keep improving with age."

"Modesty becomes you," I teased.

After Greg had left, I sat down at the table with my coffee and phone to listen to my voicemails. The first message was from our customer service department, assuring me that the listing was now live. A second message was from Riverview Bank, asking if I would like to do an open house or perhaps a broker's open, and if so, please notify them, and they would be happy to provide refreshments for the occasion. They could accommodate me on very short notice too.

This was a new one. I didn't even think the bank knew I existed. My prior listings had not exactly been ones that qualified for an elite broker's open. These were occasions when a bus or minivan full of real estate agents toured the house for sale, made suggestions, and lined up potential clients for showings.

The third call was from Tricia Hudson of Primer Properties. I grimaced when I heard her squeaky voice on the other end. Tricia and I had been participating agents on another home sale recently, and thanks to my client's antics, it had not gone well. And when my coworker turned up dead, Tricia was one of the first to accuse me of murder in cold blood. She said that she had an out-of-town buyer interested in the Steadman home, and they had a few questions. She asked me, ever so sweetly, to return her call at my earliest convenience.

I tried to contain my excitement, but it was difficult. If I sold this house, our money problems would be over for quite some time. The sale would also be tremendous for Jacques' new brokerage. It would have been perfect and more profitable if Tricia wasn't involved and Jacques and I were representing both the buyer and the seller, but it was rare to work both sides of the deal these days.

I had learned, from over three years in the real estate business, it was rare that things ever went exactly as I wanted them to.

The buzzing of my phone jerked me out of my thoughts, and I stared at the screen. "Yes, boss?"

"How are we feeling this morning, my dear?"

I yawned. "About the usual. Exhausted. I got your text, and Tricia Hudson left me a message. She has a client interested in seeing the Steadman mansion, but it may be a last minute thing. Out of towners, I guess."

Jacques giggled like a schoolgirl. "That isn't all. Susan Redwood of Houses Galore just phoned me as well. She wants to set up a showing for tomorrow."

"Wow. I didn't think there would be so much interest this fast." I raised my legs and extended them over the chair next to mine.

"The house is priced to sell," Jacques said. "Obviously Ben and Michelle are eager to move. They could have easily gone another hundred grand higher on the asking price. So that makes the mansion a virtual steal. Would you call Ben, and see if we can show it tomorrow? Are you available? Did Ben tell you if he wants one of us present at all the showings?"

"Yes, he was insistent upon that. I don't think I have anything going on for tomorrow. What time does Susan want to set up the showing for?"

"Four o'clock," Jacques replied. "And I have a closing tomorrow at two, so I'm not sure if I'll make it in time. If it ends early enough, I will definitely meet you."

"Shoot. I'm supposed to bring Darcy to get some pointers from Michelle for cheerleading. Maybe Michelle wouldn't mind if I dropped her off at the house and they rode over to the field together?"

"Darling, as long as you're there, I don't care what you have to do. And as you're well aware, it's a good idea if the sellers aren't home at the time of the showing, so please impress that upon Michelle when you speak to her. Buyers feel rushed if they know the owner is at home."

"Good grief, you act like this is my first time showing a house."

"It's not that," Jacques argued. "I have every faith in your ability. But if we can turn this around for a quick sale, it will put everything into perspective for me. And I received more good news this morning too."

"It's only eight-thirty. How long have you been at it? Have you been out jogging too?"

"Now that you mention it, Ed and I hit the gym at five this morning."

I rolled my eyes so far back in my head I was afraid I might hurt myself. "What is it with you men?"

I heard him chuckle. "Having trouble keeping up with the old man, Cin?"

"That's putting it mildly." I reached into the kitchen cabinet for a multivitamin. "Okay, I'll show the house if you call Tricia back and answer her questions. She hates my guts, and I'm really not in the mood for her phony act right now."

"Fair enough," Jacques said. "And as I said, there's more good news. Word has already leaked out about the Steadman mansion, and I have an appointment to list the Greenweld Estate this afternoon."

"Oh, that's awesome!" I squealed. "See, things are getting better already."

"Hope so, darling. Talk to you later."

After he hung up, I glanced at the wall clock. Almost nine. Was it too early to call Mr. Connors? I'd try my doctor's office first. As it turned out, Dr. Sanchez had a cancellation Wednesday morning at ten, so I was scheduled to come in then. I hoped there was some magical pill that might make me feel better. Then a tiny chill swept over me. Could there be something else wrong with me? Maybe a fatal virus?

Stop it, Cin. You're letting your imagination run away with you, as usual.

I grabbed another cup of coffee and dialed Aaron's number. It rang twice, and then a brisk man's voice answered. "Yo!"

I paused for a moment. "Hi, I'm looking for Aaron Connors."

"You've found him. You're not selling anything, are ya?"

"Mr. Connors, my name is Cindy York. I understand that you used to be a police officer in the town of Burbank, where I live?"

"That is correct, ma'am. What can I do for you?"

Just blurt it out. "About twenty-five year ago, you were one of the officers who investigated a case of apparent suicide. The victim's name was Paul Steadman. Do you happen to remember it?"

There was a long silence on the other end. "I recall it very well. But how does this concern you?"

"Paul was my best friend. I was the one who found his body."

"Ah." Silence again. "If memory serves, you had to be sedated that day."

This tidbit of information surprised me. "To be honest, I don't recall much after finding Paul's body. Over the years, I've tried to shut all the memories out. You're going to think what

I'm about to say is crazy, but I have reason to believe that Paul didn't commit suicide. I think he was murdered."

Aaron whistled. "That's a pretty serious claim, Miss York."

"I know that. But I'm *convinced* it wasn't suicide. I was wondering if you might have some free time in the next couple of days so that we could meet."

He cleared his throat. "It just so happens that I'm doing some gardening this morning. It's my passion now that I'm retired. I'm going out of town this afternoon to visit my daughter and won't be back until late tomorrow night. Would you like to come over this morning?"

This was better than I'd hoped for. "That would be terrific. Where do you live?"

"I'm just outside of Burbank in Milton Springs. The address is 15 Lambert Court. There's a brand new Starbucks just across from my road."

If anything, I knew my Starbucks. "I know where you're at. Can you give me about an hour to get over there?"

"Sure thing," he said. "I'll be in the yard. Come on back whenever you get here."

I clicked off and hurried back up the stairs. Stevie and Seth were still lying on my bed, watching cartoons. They looked up at me expectantly.

"I'm bored," Stevie said. "Can we go to the playground?"

"Not today. Guys, I need you to behave while your sister watches you for a few hours. Where is she, by the way?"

"Still sleeping, I think," Seth said. "I was gonna send Rusty in to wake her up."

"Don't you dare. I'm going to take a quick shower, and then I'll wake Darcy before I leave."

Stevie bounced on my bed. "Can we come with you to the office and see Uncle Jacques?"

"Not this time, honey. Mommy needs to go visit a police officer."

That got their attention. "Are you in trouble?" Stevie asked excitedly. "Did you sell someone a house that's falling down?"

Seth reached for the house phone on my nightstand. "I'd better call Dad."

"You'll do no such thing." I removed the phone from his hands. "Just stay put until I get out of the shower."

I brought my clothes into the adjoining bathroom, then showered and washed my hair. Afterward I quickly dressed, blow dried my hair, and pulled it back into a ponytail for some relief from the scorching heat.

"*Mother!*" Darcy screamed.

I threw open the bathroom door. Stevie and Seth were no longer in my room. I hurried down the hall and peered into Darcy's room. Rusty was lying next to her on the comforter. Stevie and Seth were giggling and pointing.

I narrowed my eyes at them. "What did I tell you two?"

"It was his idea," Seth said, pushing Stevie.

"It was not."

"It was too!"

"That's enough!" I wiped the back of my hand against the perspiration gathering on my forehead. Damn these hot flashes.

"Mother," Darcy whined, as she pulled the sheet up around her. "Please get this hairy creature off my bed."

"Come on, boy." Rusty didn't want to budge, so I picked him up and set him on the floor. He immediately attached himself to my leg while the twins' laughter resumed.

Stevie jumped up and down. "Rusty's hungry again!"

The dog looked up, and I swear he winked at me.

Darcy wrinkled her nose at her brothers. "Why didn't you drown them at birth?"

I detached Rusty from my leg and told him "No" in a sharp voice. He turned and galloped into the hallway like a small horse. At least I hadn't offended him.

"Okay, guys, go in the kitchen and grab a snack. Darcy and I will be down soon." I smoothed the covers on her bed. "I need you to watch the boys for a few hours. I have some errands to run."

Darcy glared at me as she rolled out of bed. "You *always* need me to watch them. This is my summer vacation too, remember? Why can't you call Grandma?"

I bit into my lower lip in an effort to temper my response. "You know that I'd rather not call Grandma unless it's really necessary. We don't always see eye to eye on certain things." *Or anything, for that matter.*

She snorted. "Word. How long do I have to watch them for? I want to go over to Heather's this afternoon so that we can practice some cheers."

"I won't be too long. I have an appointment to meet with someone, and then I need to stop by the office for a couple of hours. Why don't you skip practice for today? It's so hot outside. Tomorrow's supposed to cool off a bit when you meet with Mrs. Steadman."

Her face lit up at the mention of Michelle's name. "But I really want to get some more work in before I meet her. I don't want her to think I'm a total loser."

"Sweetheart, she's not going to think that. She's doing this because she loves the sport and wants to help you."

"She's like all over the internet and everything," Darcy gushed. "I mean, she could have been a Cowboys cheerleader if she wanted to. She was *that* good." She stared at me suspiciously. "How come you weren't a cheerleader in high school?"

I grinned. "Maybe because I'm not exactly coordinated and have two left feet?"

"Oh yeah, I forgot about that."

I glanced at my watch. "Okay, I need to get going. Don't leave your brothers alone for too long downstairs. You know what they're capable of. There's sandwiches in the fridge for lunch. And make sure you don't leave them unattended in the pool." It was only a three-foot, above-ground, metal, round pool Greg had easily installed last month, but it was quite a boost on humid days like this.

Darcy cast an irritated look in my direction. "Mother, I wasn't born yesterday. And when are you going to take care of Rusty's gross problem?"

"I'll call the vet and make an appointment for him next week. It's pretty obvious that he needs to be neutered and fast."

"Thank God," Darcy said in an overly dramatic tone. "If I hear Stevie yell the dog's hungry one more time, I may throw up."

My stomach muscles tightened at her words. "You're not the only one."

CHAPTER SEVEN

The drive to Lambert Court only took about fifteen
minutes, but with the excitement of the dog and the
phone call to arrange his upcoming visit to the vet, it was
almost eleven by the time I reached Aaron Connors's house. It
was a one-level, redbrick ranch with adjoining garage. I pulled
up behind a newer model Buick Regal and glanced around.

Aaron hadn't been kidding when he said he liked gardening.
There was a beautiful flower bed in front, surrounded by
colorful stones. The rose bushes he'd planted were in full bloom,
and I even spotted some tomatoes coming from a trellis near
the house.

I heard a screech in the driveway and turned around.
Jacques' convertible pulled in right behind mine, and he was so
quick to step on the brake I was afraid for a moment his car
might careen into mine.

I walked over to his vehicle. "Thanks for meeting me here.
But there was no need to drive like a maniac. Oh, wait. I forgot.
You don't know any other way to drive."

"There goes that sarcastic mouth of yours again." Jacques was
wearing a navy blue suit that I suspected was Prada. He threw

the jacket over the backseat and pushed his shirt up at the elbows. The man knew how to dress for success.

"He said for me to meet him in the backyard. Take your tie off. I'm broiling just looking at you in that outfit."

Jacques waved an impatient hand. "I'll be fine. Worry about yourself, darling. You look like you might melt on the sidewalk at any second."

I was dressed in a sleeveless blue sundress and sandals, yet Jacques looked more comfortable than I felt. The heat was again driving me to distraction. "It's the change."

"Remember this word," Jacques said. "Hormones. They'll be a lifesaver for you."

Since Jacques' listing appointment wasn't until the afternoon, I had called to see if he wanted to meet me here. After all, we weren't just real estate agents, as he'd pointed out. We were a new and upcoming detective team.

He looped his arm through mine. "Poirot and Hastings to the rescue again."

We walked past the garage and spotted a chain-link fence that ran around a small but pristine looking yard. There was a larger garden out back with almost every kind of vegetable I could think of, a metal picnic table painted red, and a hammock that hung between two trees in one corner. All of a sudden, a black-and-brown terrier appeared from nowhere, barking at us through the gaps in the fence.

"Scrappy, stop that!" A man who appeared to be in his early seventies came toward us with a gardening pick in one hand. He was wearing a pair of denim overalls and a white T-shirt littered with grass stains. His leathery face smiled as he reached over to open the gate for us. "He won't bite, don't worry. Are you Cindy York?"

"Yes." I extended my hand to shake his and then gestured toward Jacques. "This is my friend and business associate, Jacques Forte. It's very nice to meet you Mr. Connors."

"Call me Aaron." He shook hands with Jacques while I studied him. His sparse hair was grey, and he had a fine white stubble of beard growth surrounding his mouth. He was tall and wiry thin. As I continued to stare at him, a small flicker of recognition dawned. I was almost positive I remembered him from the day of Paul's death. He'd stopped to say a kind word to me. What it was, I couldn't recall though. Funny how setting eyes on him brought the memory instantly back.

"Come on over here, and sit yourselves down at the picnic table so we can chat."

We followed him across the yard, and I glanced around. Scrappy had retreated to a doghouse, also painted red, in another corner of the yard. It appeared that Aaron was in the process of planting more flower beds of some variety. "Isn't it kind of late in the summer for that?"

He chuckled. "I like to keep busy. Retirement has its perks, but some days it can drive you stark raving mad. You'll find out someday."

I wished. My real estate career was so uncertain most days I had to wonder at this point in my life if I'd ever know any type of retirement. Jacques and I sat across from him at the table while he wiped his face with a handkerchief and reached for a water bottle.

He gestured toward the bottle and then in the direction of the house. "Can I get either of you one?"

Jacques and I both shook our heads.

"No, thank you," I said. "It was awfully nice of you to meet with us on such short notice today."

Aaron took a long swig from the bottle. "Think nothing of it. I remember that case very well. Matter of fact, it did always kind of bother me. That's why I was interested in hearing your theory."

I leaned forward across the table on my elbows. "How so? I mean, how did it bother you?"

"Well, I did a background check on the kid at the time," Aaron replied. "No history of medical problems. He came from a prominent family. Wanted to be a doctor, from what I understand."

My throat tightened. "That's right. He was assisting at Burbank Hospital that summer. He was going to attend Johns Hopkins University in the fall."

"Great school." Aaron wiped his mouth with the back of his hand. "My granddaughter just finished up there."

"What was he doing at the hospital?" Jacques asked me. "Candy striper?"

I smiled. "No, he was a certified nursing assistant. It's the male equivalent to a candy striper, I believe. Or was."

"See, that's my point," Aaron said. "That's why I agreed to talk to you. I was never convinced it was suicide. But my boss didn't want to hear my theory."

I folded my hands together. "Paul's brother, Ben, didn't seem to think there was an autopsy performed. Do you happen to remember?"

Aaron nodded. "He's right. I tried to convince the parents to go ahead with it, but the mother was adamant. If memory serves, she passed not too long after him."

I noticed that my hands were trembling. "Was there anything about the bedroom that seemed off to you that day?"

The elderly man mopped at his head with the handkerchief again. "Little lady, you were there too. Did anything strike you as off?"

"I'm not sure," I said honestly. "It's so hard for me to remember. I'd even forgotten about being sedated until you mentioned it. I've spent so many years blocking it all out that I'm afraid I've been rather successful at it."

"Maybe you should check into hypnosis," Aaron said. "It could prove to be helpful."

The thought of being hypnotized unnerved me. "I-I don't

know," I stammered. "I just hoped that you could tell me something." *Anything.*

Aaron scratched his head. "Well, back then, there weren't many suicides around here. That was only the second one I ever witnessed, and I'd been on the force for over ten years by then."

"Did they call in an investigator?" I asked.

He shook his head. "The problem is that Burbank was—still is—a small town. And it was difficult to prove that your friend didn't commit suicide."

Jacques frowned. "I don't understand."

Aaron finished his water. "When we got to the Steadman place that day, you'd already called the operator for help, Miss York. The EMT team was the first to arrive. Which is a good thing, since they were trying to save his life. But the staff was brand new, and they touched things they shouldn't have. I mean, it's kind of hard to avoid doing so when you're trying to save a man's life, you know?"

"That's understandable," I said.

"Well, when I got there with my partner, your friend had already been loaded onto a gurney, and they were moving him into the ambulance. You were sitting outside with another EMT worker who was trying to console you. The entire scene—scene of the crime, as you're calling it now—had already been disturbed. The young man's body had been upset. The gun had been removed from his hand. The EMT guy couldn't remember how exactly he'd been holding it. I know the most important thing was to save the kid's life, but the whole process was handled so sloppily. Sad to say, I've seen that happen a few times during my career."

I cut my eyes to Jacques. This was turning out to be more difficult than I'd feared. "If they'd had the autopsy done, couldn't that have proven it might not have been a suicide?"

Aaron nodded soberly. "I tried to convince Mrs. Steadman, but she refused to listen. If the autopsy had been performed, yes, there's a good chance the coroner could have proven that maybe the boy hadn't shot himself with the gun."

I swallowed hard. "I wish you could have persuaded her."

He glanced at me with sympathy. "Why the sudden interest now? Something must have happened to convince you it was a potential murder after all this time."

I was baking from the heat of the overhead, blazing sun. "I found a letter from him. Let's just say it convinced me he did *not* commit suicide."

Aaron frowned. "Do you have it with you? I'd like to see it."

Ugh. This again. "It's a love letter he wrote to me." I reached into my purse and handed him the envelope. He read the note quietly and then glanced up at me.

"Sounds like he was crazy about you."

I nodded. "Now you understand what I'm talking about."

He handed the letter back to me. "What you're saying makes sense. I wish I could be of more assistance. If there was any type of evidence around from that day, it could help prove your theory. But I'm guessing the room he was found in has changed since then."

"Yes, I saw it this past weekend. Totally redone. It's the first time I'd been there since... Anyway, my boss and I are listing the house for the Steadmans."

"Really?" Aaron seemed intrigued. "Ben Steadman certainly works hard for his clients. I'll give him that. My ex-wife was one of them. I'm betting he needs the money after that scandal a couple of years ago."

This was news to me. "What scandal?"

Aaron grimaced. "There was a claim he was fooling around with a girl interning at his office. She was underage, which is what caused all the ruckus. A friend of a friend of mine knew the girl's family. Apparently, Ben offered up a ton of money so she'd keep quiet and not discredit him. I think he managed to keep it out of the papers, which is probably why you never heard anything."

I was stunned. No, this couldn't be right. Not Ben. He was a good guy. He loved his wife and daughter. Then again, what did I really know about the man? I remembered from my friendship with Paul that there had always been an intense case of sibling rivalry between the two. Paul had been the favorite, the baby, the perfect son. Paul had once confided to me that the two of them had never been close, although he would have liked to.

"Are you sure?" I asked

He nodded. "Of course I'm sure. I may be retired, but I still have my sources."

"Wow, this certainly puts things in a new perspective," Jacques said.

Aaron shrugged. "Maybe not. It isn't like this had anything to do with the death of his brother—unless somehow Ben was responsible for it."

"I'll never believe that." I spoke the words with more conviction than I actually felt. *Fooling around with an underage girl? Shame on you, Ben.*

"Well, since you were Paul's best friend, did you know of anyone who didn't like the boy? Try to think back."

I struggled to remember little details, but it was difficult after all this time. I recalled the scathing words of my fellow alums the other night. And what about the girl who'd had the crush on Paul—Rachel Kennedy? "Would you be able to help me find someone who stalked Paul back then?"

He raised his white, bushy eyebrows at me. "The kid had a stalker?"

"Well, she wasn't really a stalker," I admitted. "I don't remember her doing anything awful. Then again..."

Jacques placed a hand on my arm. "Did she try something?"

"I don't have any proof it was her," I said, "but the morning after the prom—which I attended with Paul—I went outside to find my car windshield shattered. At the time I assumed that someone was having fun at my expense and just happened to throw a rock at it during the night. But now I'm not so sure."

Aaron pursed his lips. "So this girl was crazy about Paul, and he was not interested in her."

I nodded. "He once told me that he couldn't stand her. But he tried to be nice and was always polite to her. Maybe that wasn't the way for him to go."

Aaron gestured to my purse. "Got a slip of paper in there? Give me her name, and I'll see if we can get her checked out. I'm assuming you don't know if she's married now or not?"

I shook my head. "No idea. She wasn't at the reunion the other day. I'm not even sure if she's still in town. I could ask Ben, but—"

He made a small sound, deep in his throat. "It might be best if you say as little as possible about this to Mr. Steadman."

"Why?"

"He could be a suspect. If your theory is correct, no one can be ruled out now."

"He's right, Cin," Jacques said soberly. "Just tell him enough to get by. Don't divulge more than you have to."

My mouth went dry, and I couldn't speak for a moment. I found it difficult to believe that Ben would have killed his own brother. Still, I had to admit it was a possibility. The thought, along with the intense heat, was making me ill.

"If I were you," Aaron went on, "I'd ask around at the hospital where Paul worked. I mean, they won't tell you much, with HIPAA laws and everything, but there's a chance you might be able to find out something. Do you know anyone who might have worked with Paul back then?"

I shut my eyes for a second to think and also block out the bright sun, wishing I hadn't forgotten my sunglasses. "Actually, my doctor is still there. I haven't seen him in a few years and rumor has it he's getting ready to retire. His name is Roger Sanchez. I have an appointment with him on Wednesday."

Aaron stroked the stubble on his chin. "There you go. He might be able to give you a lead. If there was anyone who didn't like the boy or so on, that is."

Jacques frowned. "But if that's so, why wouldn't anyone have come forward twenty-five years ago?"

"No reason to," Aaron said. "Like I said, I had my suspicions, but there was no proof it was murder. At the time, I begged my boss to let me do some further investigating, but he was adamant. If the parents had expressed an interest, maybe things would have gone differently."

I sighed. "It's like finding a needle in a haystack after all these years."

"Pretty much," Aaron agreed. "I wish I had dared defy my boss back then. That case has always been a regret of mine. If there's one thing I've learned from being a cop for over thirty years, you learn to rely on your gut instinct. It's never failed me."

"That's how I feel now," I murmured.

Aaron glanced down at the paper I'd given him and pushed it back toward me. "Write your cell phone number down for me. I've got a good friend over in the department. He can locate the last known address for the lady. I'll have him run a background check too."

I pushed the paper back and produced my business card from my purse, which I handed to him. "That would be wonderful. Any information you can find would be a huge help."

He nodded in reply and rose to his feet. "My pleasure."

Jacques and I took this as our cue to leave. Aaron walked us to the gate. Scrappy reappeared and accompanied us, his bushy tail wagging gleefully as if he was excited at the thought of our departure.

Aaron extended his hand. "I wish you all the luck in the

word with this, Mrs. York." He gestured to Jacques. "Did you say that this was your husband?"

I choked back a laugh while Jacques managed to hide a smile. "Uh, no. My boss."

Aaron smiled. "Sorry, my mistake. You two make a cute couple."

I bit into my lower lip for fear I might laugh. I glanced toward Jacques, who was smiling as well.

"Please keep me posted. I'm interested to see how you make out with this."

"Of course," I nodded. "Thanks for giving me a starting point."

Aaron started to walk back in the direction of the picnic table, then suddenly turned around. "A word of caution."

Butterflies danced in my stomach. "Yes?"

"Be careful. If you're right about this, the killer finally feels safe. After all, it's been twenty-five years. But now you're snooping around, uprooting things, and if the killer is still nearby, they'll get wind of this quick. Your life could be in danger and possibly your family's as well."

I hadn't really considered the scenario from his point of view before, and it scared me senseless. For a brief moment, I thought about abandoning the whole claim but knew deep down that I couldn't. If I walked away now, I'd be haunted by this forever. Still, Aaron was right. I needed to take extra precautions to ensure that my family would not be affected.

One thing I knew for certain. If the situation had been reversed, Paul would have done the same thing for me. This was my last chance to help a dear friend who had left this world far too soon.

I locked eyes with Aaron's. "I understand what you're saying, but I can't let this go. I need to know the truth."

His brown eyes were somber as he nodded. "Just watch your back, little lady."

CHAPTER EIGHT

"*Mom!*" Seth screamed.

I opened the door of my bedroom with one sandal on, carrying the other. "What's wrong?"

Seth made a beeline past me for my bathroom. "I have to go. And Darcy won't come out of the other one."

With a sigh, I walked down the hall and pounded on the door of the other bathroom. "Darcy, we have to leave shortly. I can't be late for my showing."

"Out in a minute, Mom."

The doorbell rang, and Rusty started to bark while Stevie yelled from downstairs. "I got it!"

Normally, I didn't let the boys open the front door unless I was right there with them. With the way things were shaping up, you never knew when a killer or some other type of psycho might show up on my doorstep.

This time, I knew it was only Helen. Sure, she wasn't a killer but still deadly in other ways. I'd asked Greg to call her last night to see if she could babysit. While they had been chatting, Helen made a point of asking her son if he was taking Viagra.

Greg had almost collapsed on the floor laughing when he'd told me about it later.

"Cynthia!" I heard my mother-in-law scream. "Get this thing away from me!"

I bit into my lower lip in an attempt to keep from laughing. I walked downstairs and into the living room. Fortunately, Darcy had exited the bathroom and was now behind me, because I wanted to leave as soon as possible. I detached Rusty from Helen's leg.

Helen brushed off her slacks and glared at me. "That thing is a monster."

"No he's not," Stevie argued. "He's a cookie spaniel."

"That's cocker spaniel, dear," Helen gently admonished him. She cast her eyes in my direction, and her expression changed. "What in God's name do you have on?"

I glanced down at my ivory-colored, short-sleeved blouse and purple, knee-length skirt. "I'm showing a house today."

"Not *you*. My granddaughter."

I whirled around. Darcy was dressed in a tank top and sweatpants that rode a bit low on her waist but, in my opinion, weren't revealing. "She looks fine, Helen."

My mother-in-law's nostrils flared. "Why do you keep letting my granddaughter wear such tawdry outfits?"

There was no winning with this woman. "It's not tawdry, and all the girls her age wear them."

She mumbled something under her breath that sounded like "the apple doesn't fall far from the tree."

I decided to ignore her comment. "Greg should be home within an hour." Translation in my head—*so happy I don't have to deal with you again today.*

"Good. I need to speak with him. He must be under some type of spell."

"Are you a witch, Mom?" Stevie asked.

I grabbed my purse off the hook by the front door, reached

for the knob, then held it open for Darcy to exit through first. "Ask Daddy when he comes home. Tell him Grandma wanted to know."

I shut the door quickly before Helen could add anything.

"Why does Grandma dislike you?" Darcy asked as she settled into the passenger seat.

I started the engine. "She doesn't think I'll ever be good enough for your father."

"Oh." She wrinkled her brows. "So who is good enough for him?"

"Probably no one."

As we pulled into the driveway of the mansion, Darcy gasped audibly, and her jaw almost hit the floor of the car. "She lives *here*?"

"This is the house I'm selling," I said with pride.

"Wow," Darcy breathed. "I can't wait to meet her. Did you know that the Dallas Cowboys wanted her to be a cheerleader? But she left training camp because she decided she'd rather get married and raise a family instead."

Hmm. A slightly altered version of the truth, but since there was no reason for me to belittle Michelle to Darcy, I smiled and said nothing.

"She's, like, famous," Darcy breathed. "And to think, she's your age, has a daughter older than me, and still looks gorgeous."

A faint feeling of envy rose from within, but I pushed it away. After all, the house would sell soon, and then Michelle would leave the state. It was silly to be bothered by my daughter's star-struck attitude toward Michelle.

We walked up the path to the front door, which opened before we had a chance to knock. Michelle stood there in a pair of pink sweatpants and a white Jets T-shirt. A pink headband held her blonde hair back from her face. Her emerald eyes were accented by smoky, gray eyeshadow. As usual, she looked gorgeous. She smiled at Darcy and then nodded to me. "Great to see you, as always, Cindy."

"Hi, Michelle. Thanks for letting us meet you here." I gestured to my daughter. "This is Darcy. Darcy, this is Michelle Steadman."

Michelle extended a well-manicured hand in her direction. The diamond on her left hand was massive, and I found myself wondering how her finger didn't break from the weight of it.

Darcy's face went red. "It's such an honor to meet you, Mrs. Steadman." She gave a slight curtsy.

Oh, good grief.

"The pleasure is all mine," Michelle said with a smile that struck me as a bit conceited, obviously eating up Darcy's praise. She turned her attention to me. "Wesley is out in the kitchen preparing dinner, but he won't disturb you during the showing. Ben may be home before you're done, but he'll make himself scarce in the study."

"It's really best if no one is here when I show the house," I said. "You don't want the prospective buyers to feel inhibited in any way."

Michelle nodded. "I understand completely, but I do need Wesley to prepare the meal. Maybe Darcy would like to join me for dinner, and then I could drive her home afterward?" She turned to my daughter, who looked like she might pass out from the suggestion.

"I-I don't want to impose," Darcy said and glanced at me.

"It's no imposition at all. I'd love to have you. Ben can't stay for dinner as he has meetings tonight, and I hate to eat alone." Michelle jingled her car keys. "We'll take the 'Vette, and put the top down since it's cooled off a bit. How does that sound?"

If my daughter's mouth opened any wider, I thought a swarm of bees might fly inside.

"That sounds totally awesome! Can I, Mom?" Her large, brown eyes gazed at me.

With both of them watching me expectantly, how could I refuse? "I guess that would be all right." I smiled at Michelle. "Thank you. Bring her home whenever you like. I don't want Darcy to overstay her welcome and ruin any plans you might have."

She gestured with her hand. "Oh, that's fine. I don't have any place to be tonight. I'm just your typical old married lady."

Yeah, right.

Darcy followed Michelle like a stray kitten to the garage where she beeped the door open. A minute later they zoomed past me in her bright, candy-apple-red Corvette.

Darcy waved, a huge grin plastered across her face. "Bye, Mom!"

As I dutifully waved back, a small flicker of doubt flashed through my brain, but I forced it away. I hadn't been convinced that it was a good idea to mix family with work and the biggest sale of my career. Then again, seeing Darcy so happy made it all worthwhile. She'd even bragged to some of her friends, who'd hinted about meeting Michelle as well.

Susan Redwood was prompt and punctual at four o'clock. She was an attractive woman in her early sixties with a mass of curly salt-and-pepper hair and warm brown eyes.

"Cindy, how nice to see you," she said. "I've been meaning to ask how you made out with the Tanner house."

"It came off the market last week," I said. Sadly, another missed opportunity for me. Susan had shown the house to one of her clients last month, and they'd made an offer, but my sellers wouldn't budge on their asking price. They owed almost as much as they were selling it for and needed the entire amount just to break even. I knew it had been risky to take the listing but had to try. "Since it's almost August, they're going to place it back on next spring so they don't have to uproot their kids from school. Perhaps the value will increase by then."

She nodded. "That sounds like a sensible plan."

"How did your clients make out? Did they find anything?"

Susan smiled. "Yes, a lovely house over on Brendan Avenue. Just as nice as the listing you had and for fifteen grand less."

Thanks, Susan. Let's not hit Cindy when she's down. "That's great."

She glanced at her watch. "I don't know what's keeping them. Gloria and Lila are always so prompt."

Something about the names jarred my memory. "Are they a couple?"

She laughed. "No, sisters. About my age. Neither one of them has ever married. Gloria won the lottery last month. Three million dollars. She'd already been looking for a house off and on, but after the winnings, her price range increased dramatically." She grinned. "Fortunately for me, I just happened to catch her interview on the news and stopped by her house the next day for a little chat and to offer my services."

Some people have all the luck. "How fantastic for you."

The front door opened, and someone called out, "Hello?"

I put on my best happy face and turned around to greet the two women. When my gaze met theirs, my smile instantly faded, and I fought the sudden urge to groan.

Gloria and Lila Danson. I remembered these two women well. They had been previous guests at an open house I'd hosted a few months ago for a now-deceased coworker. Back then, they'd been accompanied by their robust, brown-and-white bulldog. Sure enough, he was now situated between the two of them. He wore a black, diamond-studded collar around his thick neck with a matching leash.

"You!" Lila exclaimed. Spittle formed at the corners of her mouth. She was thick-waisted with shoulder-length, fine, white hair while her sister was more fragile looking. "I remember you. You made Sherlock leave."

As if on cue, Sherlock whined and opened his mouth, displaying several sharp, pointed teeth in the process.

"I see he's still fond of me," I said dryly.

"*She* has the listing on this house?" Gloria asked Susan. "How is that even possible?"

Sherlock growled low in this throat as I pointed at him. "Ladies, I'm sorry, but once again, he needs to go outside. No dogs allowed in the house. Your agent will tell you the same thing."

Susan stood there in silence, looking uncomfortable.

"Susan?" I prompted her.

She smiled hesitantly at me. "Maybe it would be okay just this once, for a little while. I don't see the harm in it."

I couldn't believe my ears. "You know the rules as well as I do." Then I stopped myself. Of course. Susan wanted to make a sale. She'd do anything the dog-toting, lottery-winning sisters wanted her to at this point. If necessary, she'd probably follow Sherlock around the grounds outside with a pooper-scooper. Come to think of it, maybe that wasn't such a bad idea. I wondered if dog walker paid more than what I was currently earning.

I pointed my finger at Sherlock, then at the front door. "Outside, buddy. Come on." He started to bark loudly, scaring Susan, who dropped her folder, filled with papers. Sherlock walked over to the folder and proceeded to pee on it.

"Now, Sherlock, that was very naughty." Gloria scolded him in a singsong voice.

I ran into the kitchen and asked Wesley for some paper towels and cleaner. He handed the items over and raised his eyebrows but didn't ask any questions. And that was a good thing because I really didn't want to answer them.

Just as I returned to the drawing room, the front door opened and Jacques walked in. He was dressed to the nines in a dark blue pinstripe suit, white dress shirt, and red tie. He glanced from me to the women, to the dog, and finally back to me where I sat on the floor surrounded by paper towels.

"My closing finished early ladies, so here I am." He gave the women a formal bow. "And these must be the Danson sisters. I'm Jacques Forte, owner of Forte Realty. It's always an honor to meet such lovely women as you."

Oh brother. He was really piling it on high today.

Lila's snarl quickly changed into a full-fledged grin. "My, aren't you a lady killer!"

"Indeed." Gloria giggled. "Such a charmer. And handsome too. I bet *he* won't make Sherlock leave."

From my position on the floor, I shot daggers at my boss. "The *dog*, Jacques." Jeez, was anyone going to side with me?

He presented the women with his most elegant smile. "Ladies, what my coworker, Mrs. York, might have failed to mention is that the owner has a severe allergy to any type of pet dander. I'm sure Cindy wouldn't mind taking him for a walk around the premises while I show you the rest of the house."

Such a liar. But way better than what I could come up with on the spur of the moment. And it seemed that my premonition of dog walker was about to come true.

"Well," Gloria said. "I guess that's understandable. Although I don't see how such a sweet boy like Sherlock could make anyone sick." She frowned down at me. "Are you sure you know how to handle him?"

Jacques offered me a hand up, and I rose to my feet. "Miss Danson, I have a dog myself. I'll take very good care of him. I promise."

They reluctantly handed over the leash and, without another word, followed Susan into the pristine kitchen. Jacques started in their direction, but I yanked him back by his jacket sleeve.

"Not so fast there, Mr. Charm. This is my listing, but I get stuck holding the bag?"

Sherlock whined.

"Oh, don't take it so personally," I said to the dog.

Jacques clasped his hands as if in prayer. "Cin, if they buy this house, I'll get Rusty his own diamond-studded collar. What's the deal here? Do you have some type of history with these two women?"

"They came to an open house that I hosted before. It pretty much went like this showing. The dog peed on the floor, and I had to clean it up. And Susan was no help at all. She wouldn't even think to deny those two anything."

"That's because she's pretty much scraping the bottom of the barrel like the rest of us. Please, darling, bear with me. It's still your listing. Just let me sugarcoat things a bit. I'll have those two eating out of my hand shortly."

A visual image I could have done without. "Fine. Go on, I'll take care of the dog."

Jacques blew me a kiss and hurried off to join the rest of the posse. I stared down at Sherlock, who let out a huge yawn in response.

"Yeah, the feeling's mutual, buddy."

I had my hand on the knob when it suddenly turned, and the door opened, startling me. Ben stood there in a black designer suit I could have sworn was Armani. He looked very professional and handsome. When his eyes met mine, I glimpsed Paul for a moment. The effect both shocked and saddened me.

He put his briefcase down and looked at me anxiously. "Are you okay?"

I nodded and then found my voice. "I'm sorry. You just surprised me."

He stared down at Sherlock with a confused expression. "Do you always bring your dog to showings?"

Sherlock whined and walked toward him. Ben laughed as he reached down a hand to pet him. "Love the collar. He's cute but way too fat, Cindy."

I smiled. The direct statement was another thing that reminded me of Paul. "He's not my dog. Jacques just arrived, and he's showing the house to prospective clients who brought the canine with them. I was about to take him outside."

"I'll go with you," Ben said. He removed his suit coat and tie and tossed them onto a small table that held a silver tray I assumed was for calling and real estate cards. He held the door open for me, and we proceeded toward the rear of the estate.

There was a marble-lined path that led around the entire mansion. Each side was shielded by large maple and oak trees that provided much relief from the blazing sun. One side of the mansion stretched over a small lake. I recalled sitting by it with Paul on many days like this.

As we walked along, I thought about the information that Aaron had volunteered yesterday. When Sherlock stopped to relieve himself by an oak tree, I tried to figure out how best to broach the subject. "I'd like to ask you about something, and it's kind of personal."

Ben drew his eyebrows together. "Okay."

Okay, extremely personal. "I heard there was an incident a few years back that concerned you and a former intern. A very *young* intern."

Ben opened his mouth in surprise. "Where did you hear such a thing?"

I ignored his question. "You had to shell out a lot of money to keep that hushed up, didn't you?"

His mouth compressed into a thin, fine line. "I asked you where you heard it, Cindy."

Eyes that were cold and stormy focused on my face and sent a chill through my entire body, even on a warm day like this.

I found myself concocting a lie on the spur of the moment. "Uh, I have a friend who has connections to the police department."

A muscle ticked in Ben's jaw. "Interesting. I thought you were looking into my brother's death, not my personal background. Are you suggesting that the two connect somehow? If so, perhaps Michelle and I should rethink our choice of agents for the house."

My heart sank into the bottom of my stomach. Jacques would die if we lost this sale. *Why couldn't I keep my big mouth shut?* Because I wasn't convinced that Ben didn't have anything to do with Paul's death. I was grasping at straws here, but if Ben had lied to everyone about the affair with an underage intern, maybe he had lied about other things as well.

In the meantime, I had to reassure him somehow. "Ben, you misunderstood me. I wasn't fishing around for information on you. When I happened to mention that I was selling your house, this person brought up the incident. I know that you did nothing wrong."

I'd never been good at lying but prayed I'd pull this one off.

Ben's expression was doubtful as he studied my face. "This is between you and me."

I nodded. "Of course."

"Her name was Jamie," he said dryly. "She was beautiful and quite the charmer. She would follow me around everywhere, more than anxious to do my bidding." He smiled, remembering. "It made me feel quite young again."

Ew. He was talking about a girl that was younger than his own daughter. Closer to *my* daughter's age. Gross. What the heck was the matter with him?

"She came on to me," Ben said defensively. "Plus, she lied about her age. Anyhow, one night she stayed late, helping me organize documents for an important case. I ordered dinner in for us. The next thing I knew, she kissed me."

"What did you do?" I didn't dare breathe.

His face colored. "She wanted more, and I told her no, that I was a happily married man. Unfortunately, she paid no attention and was in the process of taking her clothes off when one of my associates entered my office. They then succeeded in blabbing the tale to everyone."

Ben cleared his throat. "I panicked and told Jamie that her internship was complete and that I'd give her a great reference. She must have seen dollar signs because all of a sudden she threatened to go public with her own fictitious account of what happened, unless I helped her pay for law school. Wait, let me rephrase that. Unless I paid for *all* of her law school tuition, plus some miscellaneous expenses."

He stopped and watched me for a moment. I nodded for him to continue.

Ben stared off toward the lake. "I didn't want my business threatened or for Michelle to find out, so I agreed. I paid her some money and thought she'd go away, but she kept coming back for more. The next thing I knew, her parents were threatening to sue me, so we arranged a payoff—a very large one, in fact—for their silence. It set me back quite a few years financially."

"I see." Which was why selling the house made sense.

He stared at me pointedly. "As far as I know, Michelle has no idea what transpired. And I'd like to keep it that way. Understand?"

I got his message loud and clear. *Breathe to Michelle about this and your house listing goes away.* "Of course. I would never say anything."

He nodded. "Good. Now I'm guessing that you're done with these insinuations?"

The story sounded fishy to me and filled with loopholes. I wanted to believe him but had my doubts. Still, how could I prove it? "Yes. Thank you for telling me."

We were back by the front door. He let me enter first, then shut the door behind us and reached for my hand. Surprised, I stared at him.

"Come on back with me to my study. I have something for you. Don't worry about the dog. He can come too. Michelle isn't very fond of animals, but what she doesn't know won't hurt her."

Interesting. Was he referring to Sherlock or his potential affair?

As I followed him down the sterile hallway with Sherlock trotting beside us, I wondered if there was any way I might be able to track down his former intern. I had to assume Ben lied about her real name. Maybe Aaron would know.

We entered Ben's study. He sat down behind the massive carved-wood desk, obviously an antique, and opened the deep bottom drawer. He removed a large plastic Ziploc-type bag and handed it to me. There was a hat of some sort in it.

Ben smiled sadly. "Do you know what this is?"

I glanced curiously at it for a moment. Then I saw the familiar Mets logo on the front of the hat, and my heart almost stopped beating. "It's his—hat. Paul was wearing it when..." I handed the hat back to Ben and brought my hands to my face, trying to restrain myself from bursting into tears.

Ben put an arm around me. "I didn't mean to upset you. I thought you'd like to have something to remember him by. Had I known back then how Paul felt about you, I would have made sure you'd received a memento. This is all that's left now."

He handed the bag back to me, and I hugged it against my chest. "Thank you so much. I'll treasure it always. I can't believe you kept it all these years."

"Actually, my mother did. They brought her Paul's personal items the next day. She would have kept everything, but the clothes he was wearing were covered in blood—" He stopped himself and forced a smile. "God, he was always wearing that stupid hat."

Tears ran down my cheeks, and I brushed them away. "He loved baseball. We were supposed to go to the old Shea Stadium that summer. I have nothing from him, except the note that he wrote. You have no idea how much this means to me."

Ben cleared his throat. "Paul was always the favorite. When

he died, my mother lost all reason for living. She treated his room like a shrine. I'd forgotten all about the hat until we started prepping things for a possible move a few weeks back. I found it in an old trunk upstairs in the attic."

"I'm so glad you did."

He watched me closely. "Have you found any possible leads yet?"

I was about to respond and then remembered Aaron's words from yesterday. I forced myself to wonder if I could be looking at a potential killer. Was Ben just giving me the hat to try to fluster me? Was he hoping I'd forget about the intern story, which I figured he'd lied about? Did he have a motive for wanting Paul dead? I knew there'd been jealousy and sibling rivalry, but was that enough of a reason to take your own brother's life? Maybe there had been something else...

"Cindy?"

Ben's voice jerked me out of my thoughts. He watched me intently. I smiled and crossed my fingers underneath the bag.

"Nothing yet," I said. "But you'll be the first to know."

CHAPTER NINE

*J*t was past nine o'clock Tuesday evening and still no Darcy. I'd sent her two texts in the last hour that had gone unanswered. I'd even called the Steadman mansion but, the call had gone directly to their answering machine. I hadn't left a message.

I joined Greg in the study. He looked up from an email he was typing and pulled me down on his lap for a kiss. "Do you want me to drive over there?"

I placed my arms around his neck. "No, I'm sure she's fine. But I'm a little upset with her for not answering my texts. Let's give her another hour." I knew she'd die of embarrassment if Greg went over to the mansion. Contrary to what Darcy thought, I remembered what it was like to be a teenager.

Shrieks of laughter could be heard from the family room downstairs, followed by a loud popping noise.

With a sigh, Greg released me and got to his feet. "I'd better tell the gang to get ready for bed."

"Like they're actually going to sleep." I'd forgotten that I had promised Stevie and Seth they could each have a friend spend the night. When I had arrived home at five-thirty, I found five males—including my husband—wondering what was for dinner.

Greg kissed me again, and moments later I heard him descending the stairs to the basement. I was about to follow him when car lights reflected off the living room window. I opened the front door to blaring rock music and the sight of Darcy alighting from Michelle's Corvette.

Michelle waved to me and blew Darcy a kiss. "See you Friday, honey!"

Darcy waved back at her. "Thanks, Michelle!" She breezed past me with a large shopping bag in her hand and started for the stairs. "Hi, Mom. I'm beat. See you in the morning."

"Just a minute, young lady." I sat down on the couch and patted the seat next to me. "We need to talk."

"Sure, what's the problem?"

I struggled against the irritation that was rapidly growing inside me. "The problem is that I texted you twice, and you never responded. I was starting to worry."

Her grin faded. "I'm sorry. Michelle and I went to the mall after dinner to get some workout clothes. I guess I never bothered to check my phone."

Well, that was a first for my daughter. Whenever she went anywhere with me, the cell never left her hand.

Darcy's face lit up again. "Guess what? We're going to get together Friday and do some more practicing, then have lunch at the Country Club. She said we'll make a whole day of it. She's so awesome."

"Who's awesome?" Greg was leaning against the doorway, watching us.

Darcy got to her feet and ran over to hug her father. "Michelle Steadman. I mean, she's like the coolest person I've ever met."

The irritation that had settled in the bottom of my stomach had a new name—jealousy. I knew it was ridiculous, but I couldn't quite make the sensation go away.

Greg pointed at the shopping bag. "What's in there?"

"Uh, it's some workout clothes and sneakers for practicing. Michelle said they were top of the line and could really make a difference in how I perform," Darcy stammered.

I bit into my lower lip. "Did you use your babysitting money to pay for them?"

She hesitated a second too long. "Uh, no. Michelle said they were a gift from her."

That was the last straw. I got to my feet and crossed the room, my tone low and strange to my own ears. "You know we don't want you accepting gifts like that. You will return them to her as soon as possible."

Darcy's face was crestfallen. "I didn't *ask* for them, Mother. Michelle insisted on buying them for me."

"You have plenty of outfits you can wear for practice. You will return them to her the next time you see her, or I will."

Darcy's nostrils flared. "*You* were the one who asked her to help me. And you're getting money from her too."

My mouth opened in surprise. "I'm selling her house. That's a business deal and completely different."

She tossed her head. "Yeah, right. You're just jealous because you're not the athletic type. And don't be angry at her because she's talented and beautiful."

For a moment, I thought this must be someone else speaking, not my kind and wonderful daughter. Where was all of this coming from?

Greg stepped forward and held out his hand for the bag. "You spent a few hours with a complete stranger today, and all of a sudden, she's more important than your own mother?"

Darcy's lower lip trembled. "I didn't say that."

I muffled a laugh. "Okay, Darcy. You win. I gave birth to you and have taken care of you for sixteen years, but Michelle understands you better. Hey, it makes sense to me."

Her face turned crimson. "Michelle *does* know. You don't realize how competitive this sport can be. She used to coach her daughter, and she totally gets it. Wow, Paula is *so* lucky." She threw the bag on a chair and ran upstairs. Seconds later, we heard the door to her room slam.

I opened the bag and flinched when I saw the price tags of the items. There were several hundreds of dollars of clothing in there. I shut the bag and sank down in the chair next to it.

Greg's expression was grim. "She owes you an apology."

"Forget it." My voice shook.

He pulled me out of the chair and into his arms. "Baby, what's wrong?"

I relayed the story of Ben and the intern as gently as I could. A muscle ticked in my husband's jaw, and his eyes blazed, but I was quick to put his mind at ease.

"Don't worry. He wasn't home tonight," I said. "But now, Darcy's made plans with Michelle for Friday, and I'm uneasy about her spending any more time with either of them. Plus, who knows if Ben could have been involved with Paul's death somehow?"

Greg hugged me tightly to him. "If that scumbag was carrying on with a minor, I don't want him anywhere near our daughter, and that goes for his wife too. Just tell Darcy you need her to watch the boys on Friday. Problem solved. Next week, she won't even remember who Michelle is."

I leaned my head on his shoulder. "One minute everything is fine, and the next minute she's all ticked off at me. And those mood swings of hers. Ugh. Compared to her, the twins are a piece of cake."

He cupped my face in his hands and smiled. "It's just a phase she's going through. Now, I haven't met the quote, 'talented and beautiful Mrs. Steadman,' but I know she can't possibly be as good-looking as my wife is."

I smiled up at him. "Well, Michelle *is* gorgeous."

"She sounds way too artificial. You're the real deal, baby."

How did I ever get so lucky? I kissed Greg lightly across the lips. "You always know how to make me feel better."

He grinned, and his hand went to my backside. "That's not the only thing I'm good at."

"Okay, you need to behave. We have guests here. Plus, I have a doctor's appointment in the morning and really need some sleep. Rain check?"

He sighed and released me. "All right, but don't get used to it."

"CAN'T Tyler and Kevin stay here with us today?" Stevie pleaded with a mouthful of scrambled eggs. "We'll be good. I promise."

I drained my coffee cup. "No, Daddy's going to drop them off at their houses on his way to work."

"Can I have some more eggs and bacon?" Kevin asked. His family was new to the area, and this was the first time he'd been to our house. He was a robust boy who probably weighed as much as both the twins put together. He'd managed to consume five pieces of pizza to everyone else's two slices last night. I had planned to save the remaining pizza for the twins' lunches today, but the rest had mysteriously disappeared overnight.

As I reached for the pan on the stove, Greg, who had been standing at the counter reading the paper and drinking his coffee, leaned over and whispered in my ear. "I don't think you should give him any more food. He's going to make himself sick."

I stared at my husband in amazement. "What do you want me to do? I can't refuse the kid if he's hungry."

"I hope he's an only child," Greg muttered. "He'd kill our food budget, hands down."

I grabbed the platter on the counter and refilled Kevin's plate. The other boys watched in fascination as Kevin shoveled the food into his mouth.

"Awesome," Seth breathed.

"Really sweet, man," Stevie agreed.

"Can't I stay?" Kevin looked up at me pleadingly as he munched away.

I placed my cup in the sink. "I'm sorry, Kevin. I have a doctor's appointment this morning, and Mr. York has to go to work."

"Don't you work?" he asked as he downed another glass of milk.

I made a mental note to stop at the grocery store after my appointment. "Yes, I'm a real estate agent."

"She finds dead bodies!" Tyler Croger told his friend. He'd been a classmate of the twins since kindergarten, and also lived in our development. "She was almost a murderer once, too."

I was confident I'd be getting a phone call from Kevin's parents later in the day. "Okay, guys, everyone upstairs to brush their teeth so you'll be ready to go when Mr. York leaves."

Greg placed the paper down on the counter and scanned the room. "What happened to my briefcase? Did you kids move it?"

"Um." Seth looked at his twin with apprehension.

Greg folded his arms across his chest and tapped his foot. "Um what? Where is it?"

Stevie glanced up sheepishly at his father. "We kind of borrowed it last night to play *Law and Order*."

My husband pointed in the direction of the stairs. "Go find it. *Now.*"

Stevie got to his feet and ran out of the room, with Kevin barreling after him. "Wait for me! I want to go too!"

I heard them lumbering up the stairs and turned to Seth. "Go make sure your sister is out of bed. And do not bring Rusty in there again."

He nodded and raced out of the room.

Greg gave me a swift kiss. "I can't wait for these kids. I've got a nine-thirty meeting and will barely make it at this rate."

I sighed. "Just go. I'll take them home."

"Mom!" Stevie screamed. "Come quick!"

Fearing the worst, I ran for the stairs with Greg at my heels. "What is it?"

Stevie appeared in the doorway of his room with a horrified expression. "Kevin just threw up all over my bed."

I groaned and smacked my head with the palm of my hand. "Please let this be a bad dream."

Kevin appeared before me, a streak of vomit running down the front of his shirt and a dazed look on his face. I stared at the puddle on the bed and then started to gag myself. I ran out of the room and bumped into Greg.

"She's got a weak stomach," I heard Seth say to his friend.

"You were right," I told my husband and covered my mouth.

He sniffed at the air and made a face. "Go find him something to wear. I'll clean up the mess."

My husband was truly one in a million. I ran downstairs, grateful to leave the room, and rummaged through the clean clothes in a basket by the washer until I found a sweatshirt I thought might fit Kevin. True, it was almost eighty degrees outside, but I couldn't send the kid home in the shirt he'd been wearing. I ran back upstairs, ushered Kevin into the bathroom, and gave him a washcloth to clean his face off. In a few minutes, he was good to go, and the smell had improved significantly.

Greg met me in the hallway. "I called the office to say I'd be late. Stevie's bedding is in the washer. I'll drop the monsters off at their houses. You'd better get going, or you'll be late for your appointment."

I put my arms around his neck and kissed him. "You're a life-saver. What would I ever do without you?"

"You can make it up to me tonight." Greg whispered, a sly smile on his face.

By some miracle, I managed to reach Dr. Sanchez's office right at ten o'clock. The waiting room contained about four or five other women, two were noticeably pregnant. I had no sooner given my name and sat down when a nurse opened one of the adjoining doors and called my name.

When I reached her, she pointed immediately to the scale in the corner without comment.

"Oh, right. My favorite part."

The nurse gave me a small, tired smile. She probably heard that line at least twenty times a day.

I kicked off my shoes and stepped on the scale. As suspected, I'd gained weight—six pounds to be exact. I groaned inwardly. Time to go on a diet.

She ushered me into an exam room and took my blood pressure. Just as she was finishing up, Doctor Sanchez walked in. He was in his late sixties but still an attractive man for his age. He'd delivered me and been my mother's primary physician up until the day she'd passed away from cancer. He had dyed-dark hair with a well-trimmed beard to match and warm gray eyes.

He smiled and held out his hand. "Cindy, it's been a long time. How are you feeling?"

"Well, that's why I'm here. I haven't been myself lately and—" God, I hated having to say this. "I think it's the change."

Doctor Sanchez stroked his beard as he read my chart. "Hmm. Are you tired a lot?"

I nodded. "All the time."

"When was your last cycle?"

I thought back. "About two months ago. I usually skip one a couple of times a year."

Doctor Sanchez nodded. "Not uncommon, especially at your age. Do you remember how old your mother was when she went through the change?"

"Probably about my age." Right after she'd started menopause, they'd discovered she had breast cancer. My mother had put up quite a fight, but she'd been Stage Four by that time, and the doctors had told me there was no hope. She'd passed away a few months later.

I tried to steady my nerves. "You don't think it could be related to breast cancer, do you?"

He smiled and patted my arm reassuringly. "When was your last mammogram?"

"About six months ago." I wasn't consistent about the physicals but did make the extra effort to have an annual mammogram. If only my mother had been diligent about them, the end results might have been different for her.

"Hmm, you've always had stomach issues. But these bouts of nausea… Are they worse than usual?"

"Well, yes," I admitted. "It used to be once a week. Now it's every day."

He wrote something on my chart. "I understand your concerns about the breast cancer, but there aren't usually any signs. Plus, we've made sure to monitor you closely because of your family history. I do think you could be in the early stages of menopause. You seem to have all the symptoms."

I sighed. It was hell to get old.

Dr. Sanchez studied my chart again. "I'll have my nurse come in, and we'll draw some blood to rule any other possibilities out. And I see that you had an internal exam when you had your mammogram."

"That's right."

He tapped his pen against the folder. "There is a chance that you might have an ulcer."

I hadn't thought of this possibility and leaned forward. "So, it may be an ulcer instead of menopause?"

Doctor Sanchez laughed. "I've never seen someone excited about the prospect of having stomach problems before."

"Well, in my opinion, it beats the other thing hands down."

Dr. Sanchez positioned the chart underneath his arm. "Sit tight. My nurse will be in shortly. Good seeing you. Tell Greg I said hello."

I stopped him before he could reach the door. "Um, Doctor, I was wondering if you remembered Paul Steadman? He worked at Burbank Hospital with you one summer, many years ago."

A look of surprise crossed his face. "Of course I remember him. Nice boy. What a shock when he killed himself."

Suddenly, I felt foolish. "Paul was my best friend. And I'm convinced he did *not* commit suicide."

The doctor raised his eyebrows in confusion. "Cindy, what are you getting at?"

I hesitated for a moment. "I think he was murdered and want to know why."

He stared at me in disbelief. "This is some type of joke, right?"

I figured this might be his reaction. "I've never been more serious in my life. I know this must sound crazy, but I was wondering if you remembered anything strange going on with him, right before he died."

Doctor Sanchez shook his head. "I was just as surprised as anyone else. Paul was a good kid. I thought he had his head on straight. Of course, he'd only been at the hospital for a few weeks. But my former nurse, Mildred Reynolds, knew his family well. Before she worked for me, she assisted their primary physician, Clyde Barrows, for years."

"Is Doctor Barrows still practicing?"

Doctor Sanchez gave me a wan smile. "He passed away about a year ago. But Mildred is still around. She suffered a stroke and is wheelchair-bound but, other than that, doing fine. She lives over in Saugersville."

"That's about an hour away," I murmured more to myself. "Do you think she'd be willing to talk to me?"

"I'm sure she'd love the company. From what I hear, she has no family and gets lonely. I'm ashamed to say I haven't been out to see her in quite a while. I'll have my receptionist give you her number."

I reached for my purse on the back of the chair. "Like I said, Doctor, I'm convinced it wasn't suicide. If you know of anything that would help, no matter how irrelevant it would seem, I'd appreciate you sharing it with me."

Doctor Sanchez was silent as he considered. "I didn't see him the day of his death. I left on vacation that morning. I can't remember if he was scheduled to work that day or not. Sorry."

"Did you see him the day before? Was he behaving normally, or did he seem upset about something? Did he do anything that seemed odd to you? Whatever you can think of would be a huge help." I knew it was probably a futile effort and tried not to sound desperate, which of course I was.

He scratched his head. "Now that you mention it, I do remember seeing him at the hospital the day before. I'd already made my rounds, but I came back later that evening to check on a patient. And I overheard two people in one of the vacant rooms, arguing. One of the voices belonged to Paul. The other one was a woman's."

My heart hammered inside my chest. "Did you see her?"

He shook his head. "They were loud, and I was afraid they'd disturb the patients. I opened the door and found Paul standing there. She must have been hiding in the bathroom, because I'm positive I heard two voices."

"Did you ever tell the police about this?" I asked.

"Cindy, no one ever asked me. Like I said, I left on vacation the morning of his death and don't believe there was much of an investigation, if any. I assumed at the time he was just having a disagreement with his girlfriend. Since no one asked me for information, I never mentioned it."

Finally, something to go on. "He didn't have a girlfriend. Do you remember details of their conversation? Anything at all?"

Doctor Sanchez stared up at the ceiling for a moment. "I can't be positive—it was so long ago—but I do believe he might have said something to the effect of 'I won't let you do it.' Like I told you, I assumed it was a lover's quarrel. When I entered the room, I demanded Paul lower his voice, and that was the end of it. He sought me out later that night to apologize. I asked him if everything was okay, and he said, 'It will be.'"

Now, I was confused. I knew Paul hadn't been dating other girls, and the note he'd left convinced me that he wasn't pursuing anyone else. Or was he? So what had he meant by those words? And who was the woman with him?

Doctor Sanchez opened the door. "I'm sorry, Cindy, but I have another patient waiting. I'll leave Mildred's number out front for you. Call me tomorrow, and we'll have your test results ready."

I nodded and thanked him. I went out to the front desk and retrieved my receipt and Mildred's phone number. I stepped into my vehicle and reached inside the glove department for a pad of paper, jotting down some notes from our conversation. The way my memory was lately, I needed all the help I could get. I glanced at my cell and realized I had a voicemail. I played back the message, praying that there were no more catastrophes at home to contend with.

"Cindy, Aaron Connors here. The information you wanted—well, I've got it. Rachel Kennedy. Four Windsor Place, Burbank. Single, two grown children. Still in town. And—a prior arrest for… Guess what? Stalking a woman. If you go to see her, please take someone with you. And call me if I can help."

I sat there with the engine running, glancing out across the parking lot. Could Rachel have been the woman Paul had been arguing with in the hospital that evening? I wasn't positive but had become fairly certain of one thing. If I could find out the identity of this mystery woman, I might have my answer to who was responsible for my friend's death.

CHAPTER TEN

*D*octor Sanchez's office building was located across the street from Burbank Hospital, so after checking in with Darcy—who assured me everything was fine in a snide tone—I decided a little side trip was in order to see if my good friend, Melanie Flowers, happened to be working today.

I went first to the main desk of the emergency room. There were three people seated, waiting to be seen. One young man had a towel wrapped around his hand. I didn't see any blood and decided this must be a positive sign. An elderly woman sat on the other side of the room, head in hands, as the man seated next to her rubbed her back. I watched them with pity, wondering what her ailment was and feeling about a hundred years old myself.

The woman behind the glass partition opened the window and smiled. "How can I help you?"

"I'm a friend of Melanie Flowers," I lied, "and was wondering if she's working today."

She nodded. "Oh, yes. You just missed her actually. She took an early lunch."

"Shoot. Any idea when she'll be back?"

"I doubt she went far," the woman said. "She usually eats in the cafeteria downstairs. You'll probably find her there."

"Terrific. Thanks so much." I made my way back to the elevator and pressed *B* for the basement. When I exited, I spotted the sign for the cafeteria to the right. From the doorway, I peered inside the room. The place was almost deserted. A woman stood at the register, paying for her food, while a couple chatted quietly over their meal. Two men in white doctor coats were deep in discussion over coffee. At a corner table sat Melanie, her head bent over a book.

I made my way over to her table and stood at her side until she looked up. When she did, her eyes widened with surprise. "Well, look who's here. Did you just happen to be in the neighborhood?"

"Actually, I had a doctor's appointment and came down for a quick cup of coffee."

Melanie's lips curved upward into a slight smile. "Sure you did. No one wants this coffee, honey, unless you're fond of mud. You don't really expect me to buy that, do you?"

I was such a horrible liar. "Well, when I saw you in here, I was hoping that we could talk for a moment and—you know, catch up on some things. We didn't have much of a chance at the reunion."

She closed the book and set it aside. I noticed it was the *Fifty Shades of Grey* trilogy. "Oh, what the heck. Sit down. I've already read this many times. How about you?"

I slid into the seat across from her. "I don't have much time for reading these days."

Melanie brought her hamburger to her mouth and took a small bite. "Bet it's not your cup of tea anyway."

She was right, but I only smiled and decided to avoid the subject. "I like your hair color. When did you change from blonde?"

She laughed. "God, it has to be about ten years now. And for the record, what they say isn't true. Redheads have way more fun than blondes."

"I'll have to remember that, in case I ever decide to try it."

Melanie dipped a french fry in ketchup. "You disappeared pretty quickly the other night. You and your—ah—coworker. Or so you said."

Here we go again. "I wasn't feeling well, so we decided to go home early."

"Hmm." She wiped at her mouth with a napkin. "Thought maybe you two took a side trip to a hotel or something."

What was with this woman? "If possible, could you get your mind out of the gutter for one second? I'm happily married, thank you."

Melanie waved a hand dismissively. "Oh, whatever. Loosen up, honey. You've got a stick up your butt, just like your old dead pal."

Here was the opening I'd been looking for. "Why did you hate Paul so much?"

"I never said I hated him." Recognition slowly dawned on her face. "Wait a minute. That's why you're here, isn't it? You want to know if I was sleeping with him or something like that."

I debated about how much to tell her. "No. That thought never crossed my mind. I just have some unanswered questions about his death, that's all."

She sipped her Coke. "That's because in your mind I was never good enough for the Steadman studs. Well, think again."

My mouth fell open in surprise. "What are you trying to say? *Were* you sleeping with Paul?"

"No. Now, his brother, on the other hand..." Melanie smacked her lips. "He knew how to please a lady back then. Bet he still does."

No way. "Okay, so you expect me to believe that you were fooling around with Ben? Sorry, I can't see it."

She shot me a bitter smile. "Like I said. You thought you

were the only one good enough for them. You and Paul were thick as thieves for years. How long were you carrying on with him?"

I pressed my lips together in annoyance. "It wasn't like that between us."

Melanie narrowed her eyes. "Why can't you admit that you had it bad for him? I hate to burst your bubble, but Paul was just like his brother. He had others on the side, if you get my drift. So you see, it wasn't all about *you*." She slid out of the seat, leaving her dirty dishes on the table. "I need a cigarette before I go back to work. You can tag along if you want."

In silence, I followed her to the elevator, wondering what exactly her problem was. Was it just a clear cut case of envy for the Steadmans or something else? We took the elevator to the ground floor and then proceeded through the main entrance to the outside parking lot. I sat next to her on the metal bench but put as much space between us as possible. The smoke was making me nauseated.

Melanie blew a perfect circle right at my head. "You don't look so good, honey. Is that why you came to the doctor today? Is it cancer?"

Boy, she was something else. There was no way I'd share my menopause concerns with her. "I'm fine. So, how did you know Paul was seeing someone?"

She closed her eyes and inhaled deeply. "Well, I don't know for sure. But I did overhear him talking to that nurse a couple of days before he died... Old what's-her-face. She worked for Doctor Sanchez until she got sick. Paul had known her since he was a kid. He once mentioned that she previously worked for his family's physician."

"Mildred Reynolds," I breathed.

She looked at me in wonder. "That's right. How'd you know? Oh, I forgot. You guys were attached at the hip. He probably told you everything."

No, not everything. If that had been the case, maybe I could have somehow prevented what happened to him. "What did he ·say to Mildred?"

She stubbed the cigarette out on the ground, ignoring the ash receptacle that was only a foot away from her. "I'm not stupid. What are you really after? There's something else going on here."

Time to come clean, but I was only telling her what was absolutely necessary. "I'm wondering if his death might not have been a suicide."

Her mouth fell open in amazement, and a swear word popped out. "Are you serious? Why would you think that now, after all these years?"

"I've just never felt comfortable with that outcome. It might sound crazy, but I need to satisfy my curiosity. So if you heard or saw anything out of the ordinary, I would really appreciate your sharing it with me."

Melanie glanced at me sharply, obviously wondering if I was leveling with her. Then she shrugged. "I was snooping around. Mildred and Paul were in the back office, talking in hushed voices. He was asking her about male sterility and stuff like that."

This was the last thing I expected to hear. "What? You must have heard wrong."

She shook her head and shot me an arrogant smile. "So you see, your little friend wasn't as pure as you thought. He must have been getting some."

I locked eyes with her. "I told you, we weren't involved in a romantic way. This doesn't make any sense."

"How so?"

Damn. I doubted I could trust her, but she had given me a lead to go on. "Paul wrote me a letter the day before he died. He said that he was in love with me. That he always had been."

"You just told me you weren't involved with him."

"We weren't a couple. I didn't know about his true feelings until recently. So the conversation doesn't make sense if he was in love with me, like he claimed."

Melanie looked at me in disbelief. "How long have you been married, honey?"

I wasn't sure where this was headed. "Eighteen years."

She tilted her head back and laughed. "And you still don't know anything about men."

"I'm sorry?"

With a slight shake of her head, Melanie reached for a match to light another cigarette and then inhaled. "Were you sleeping with Paul?"

"Good God, for the millionth time, no!"

She sighed. "Too bad you missed out. You've obviously led a sheltered life. Trust me—it's obvious I know much more about men. It doesn't matter if he was in love with you. He had a chance to get a little booty on the side, so he went for it."

I drew my eyebrows together. "That doesn't sound like Paul's style."

She waved her hand in an impatient gesture. "Please. That's *all* men's style. And it was his brother's style too until he was forced to marry Michelle."

I watched her face closely. "So you did sleep with Ben?"

Melanie grinned. "Guilty as charged. I don't know about Paul, but if he was anything like his brother in the sack, you really missed out, honey."

Cripes. This woman was loathsome. And the more I discovered about Ben made me realize I wasn't particularly fond of him either. "Was this an ongoing thing between the two of you?"

She shook her head. "Afraid not. It only happened once. He and Michelle had a huge fight, and rumor was they'd broken up. Anyhow, I was invited to attend a party at his fraternity by a mutual friend. We started talking, then wound up back in his room. Man, I was sweating bullets for a few days afraid I might turn up pregnant, but thankfully, no."

"How lucky for you," I murmured. "So how long were you carrying on?"

"It told you, it was just that one time. The next day, he got back together with Michelle, and before long, she was pregnant." She smiled. "Man, how I longed to tell her the other night, just to see the look on her face. It would have been priceless."

I cocked my head to the side. "That's the real reason you went to the reunion, isn't it? Because you wanted to rub salt in her wounds?"

"Maybe." Melanie shrugged. "But I ended up keeping my mouth shut anyway. After our night together, Ben never gave me the time of day again. I went up to him once while he was at a softball game with Michelle. He pretended he didn't even know who I was. They both looked down at me like I was dirt." She gritted her teeth. "No one treats me that way."

"Do you think Paul could have been involved with Rachel Kennedy?"

She chuckled. "The cheerleader turned stalker? Damn, she was hot for him. Why would you bring her up now?"

"I don't know. She's all I can think of."

"Maybe if Paul was comatose, he'd have let Rachel take advantage of him. He couldn't stand that psycho. She even showed up at the hospital a few times looking for him. Paul used to hide out back and ask me to lie to her that he wasn't working."

Was there another woman in Paul's life I hadn't known about? Maybe like Ben and Melanie, he'd had a one-time fling with someone? Or could he have been drunk one night, and Rachel managed to catch up with him? Maybe Melanie was right, and I hadn't known him as well as I'd thought.

Every guy at that age had a one-track mind. Or did they? Paul had never laid a finger on me. I wasn't sure what to think anymore. I didn't like Melanie, but there was a good chance that she was telling the truth. I'd have to talk to Mildred as soon as possible to see what details she could provide.

Melanie stubbed out her second cigarette on the ground and rose from the bench. "I've got to get back to work."

"I appreciate your time," I said.

She studied me carefully. "You know what bugged me about Paul, besides the fact that he thought he was better than everyone else? The guy obsessed about everything. He always wanted to know who, what, when, and why. Mr. Twenty Questions. Totally annoying."

"That's what makes for an excellent doctor."

"Yeah, but maybe it led to his demise too. Think about it. What if he couldn't deal with the pressure of having a stalker, a so-called best friend who wouldn't put out, and was afraid he'd choke at med school?" Melanie tapped her forehead with her finger. "I'm pretty good at all that psychological crap."

Yeah, it shows. "Thanks for your help."

She smirked. "Good luck. You're gonna need it, honey."

I watched as she disappeared through the revolving doors of the entrance. Who the heck was she to call someone else a psycho? As far as I was concerned, Melanie Flowers was borderline nuts herself.

I grabbed my car keys out of my purse and noticed that I had two missed texts and a phone call from Jacques. The first text was from an hour ago. I'd placed my phone on mute in the doctor's office and forgotten to change it back. Great.

Tricia Hudson has a client who wants to see the house. Today. In one hour. I know—she pulls this crap on purpose. Ben said it's fine. Meet me there?

The next text was from five minutes ago. *We're all here. You're not. Get here. Now.*

Ugh. If I screwed this up, Jacques would hate me forever. I made a wild sprint for my car, dashing off a quick *On my way* text as I ran. I drove over the speed limit, something I never did, but with the lunch hour traffic, it still took me almost twenty minutes to arrive at the Steadman mansion. I pulled up in the driveway and spotted Jacques' convertible, Tricia's Audi, and a BMW I assumed belonged to the potential buyers. My beat-up Honda looked sadly out of place.

I smoothed out my skirt, grateful that I hadn't worn jeans to the doctor's office, and ran up the steps. The front door was unlocked, and I hurried down the hallway, still not seeing anyone. Muffled voices could be heard from above, so I climbed the stairway. When I reached the top, I was perspiring, and my stomach felt like a dead weight. Menopausal *and* out of shape. What a wonderful combo.

Jacques, Tricia, and a couple about my age were standing in the master bathroom. The room was done in a powder-blue marble stone and had a sunken glass bathtub with skylights above it. I'd never seen anything like this before. The tub was situated over the lake that ran behind the mansion. One felt like they were bathing among the tree tops. I almost had to restrain myself from jumping in to cool off my overheated, hot flash-filled body.

They all turned at once in my direction, and I saw their faces register with alarm. *Was something showing? How bad did I look?*

Tricia faked a smile. "Hello, Cindy. Allow me to present Jonah and Julie Whitaker. He's a movie producer." She spoke in a manner that suggested I should be impressed with that fact. "They're very interested in Ben and Michelle's home."

I extended my hand to both of them. "It's very nice to meet you. I'm sorry. I had an appointment on the other side of town and got here as quickly as I could."

They smiled politely and then walked past me back into the bedroom. After a sharp glance at me, Jacques followed, and I heard him say something about the lighting. The four of them chattered on. From the doorway of the bathroom, I watched them as they continued talking, aware that I'd been a temporary distraction, like a fly on the wall.

Um, hello, who does this listing belong to again?

At that particular moment, the irritation in my stomach turned into something else. I covered my hand with my mouth and swallowed the bile that was rapidly rising in my throat. *Not now. Please, not now.*

Tricia was asking Jacques about the age of the roof, and he responded, but his cautious eyes kept darting back to me. Finally, he cleared his throat nervously. "Why don't the three of you go out to the terrace, and we'll meet you there in a minute? I need to speak to Cindy about a closing this afternoon."

Tricia's phony smile lit up the room. "Of course."

Without even a backward glance at me, Tricia and her clients departed the room. Jacques waited until they were out of earshot and could be heard descending the stairs. Then he grabbed my arm. "What the heck is the matter? You're bright green. You're doing a fabulous imitation of the Wicked Witch of the West, darling."

"I...oh." I made a wild dash back into the bathroom. I couldn't reach the toilet in time but did manage to miss the floor and throw up in the marvelous glass tub instead.

Jacques knelt beside me and held my head while I retched uncontrollably for a few more minutes. I remained suspended over the side, my head resting against the cold glass, waiting for all to be right with my world again. When I looked up, Jacques carefully applied a cold, wet washcloth to my forehead. He gently lowered me to the floor and then found a bath towel in the cabinet that he rolled up and placed behind my head.

"Lie still, dear," he murmured. "I'll be back in a few minutes."

I shut my eyes and must have drifted off for a minute, because I remembered nothing until another cool cloth was being dabbed against my cheeks. I opened my eyes to see Jacques bending over me.

"How are we feeling, love?"

"Better." With his help, I managed to struggle into a sitting position.

Jacques took his jacket off and rolled up his shirt up at the elbows. He glanced at me anxiously while he cleaned out the tub. "I'm really worried about you."

"I'm sorry. I got here as fast as I could. I was at the hospital."

His expression was grim while he dried his hands. "Are you sick? Is it cancer? Tell me the truth."

"Calm down. The doctor ran some tests. I still think it's the change, but he said there's a very good chance I might have an ulcer."

"Well, with the life you lead, that certainly makes sense," he said dryly.

"I'm so sorry. Please don't be mad at me."

He rose to his feet and placed both hands on his hips. "Cin, forget about the house for a minute. I just want to make sure that you're okay. You obviously have some kind of health issue going on, and this whole incident with Paul can't be helping either."

I rose to my feet unsteadily, Jacques' arm supporting me. "Maybe not, but I have to follow through." Then I proceeded to tell him about my meeting with Melanie.

Jacques handed me an Altoid. "You need about a dozen, but this is all I have right now."

"Gee, thanks." I popped it into my mouth.

"So do you think Paul was worried he couldn't have children? Is that why he was discussing the sensitive issue with Mildred?"

"I haven't the slightest idea. But I want to drive over to her apartment and see if she'll speak to me. It's about an hour away."

Jacques glanced at his watch. "It's past noon. Let me drive you. We'll drop your car off at your house on the way."

"Do you have time?" I was secretly thrilled that he had

offered, as I wasn't crazy about taking a long drive by myself right now.

"I'm showing a house to a client at four, but other than that, I'm free. What about your schedule?"

"Darcy's with the boys, and Greg will be home early, so I'm good to go."

He frowned. "I mean, what about *your* clients? How come Barney hasn't been around?"

"Oh, didn't I tell you? He left me a message last night. He's decided to hold off on buying a house for a while. He wants to wait until the market gets better."

Jacques gnashed his teeth together. "I knew that guy was a waste of precious space and time. I should send him a bill for that chair. Well, no matter. Tricia's confident that this couple is going to make an offer. I told her to call you, since you're the agent of record. So please make sure to keep your phone close for the next twenty-four hours or so. Even at three in the morning. Place it between you and your man when it's time for bed. You know how that chick operates."

I blew out a breath. "Consider it done. Gee, that would be awesome if they do make an offer. And I promise, Jacques, I'll be on my game from now on."

"Darling, how many times do I have to tell you—I'm not worried about that. Okay, well, maybe a little. But I know how much you want this sale too. With a little luck on our side, things will be in the bag. Nothing can go wrong now."

CHAPTER ELEVEN

*M*ildred Reynolds was excited when I phoned from the car and asked if we could stop by for a visit. Jacques pulled up in front of a two-story, white, vinyl-sided home with a large wooden front porch and shutters painted light blue. Mildred had relayed to me that she lived on the bottom floor while a young, not terribly friendly couple who played loud rock-and-roll music resided above her.

As we exited the convertible, I saw one of the curtains move in the lower front window. When we reached the porch, Mildred was already positioned in the doorway, seated in her wheelchair.

"Are you Candy?" she pointed at me.

We crossed to the porch, and Jacques waited for me to ascend the steps first. I held out my hand to the elderly woman. "No, Mildred. I'm *Cindy*. It's very nice to meet you."

She gave me a wide grin, displaying several crooked teeth. Mildred was little more than a stick figure, with gray hair gathered in an untidy bun and sunken cheeks in a well-lined face. Her brown eyes sparkled as they fixed on Jacques. "And who is this handsome young man? Your husband?"

Sheesh. What was with everyone thinking Jacques and I were a couple lately?

Jacques reached for her hand. "Hello, Mrs. Reynolds. I'm Jacques Forte, a friend of Cindy's. It's wonderful to meet you."

Mildred flushed with pride. "Such lovely manners." She rolled the chair backward so that we could enter the house. "You just missed Louise. She's my aide and comes in everyday to see if I need anything. She does my grocery shopping too, which is a huge help. Tomorrow, Louise will come early in the morning and help me bathe. You two want something to drink?"

Jacques and I both shook our heads. "We can't stay long," I said.

She pushed her chair next to the small loveseat and patted its arm. "Come sit down next to me. Right here."

We sat side by side on the plush couch, and I glanced around. The room was small but tidy. The television was tuned in to a soap opera that I recognized immediately as *Days of Our Lives.* There were some family photos on the coffee table and on the wall. I pointed at one of two little girls. "Are they yours?"

She smiled. "No, that's me and my sister when we were younger. I never married and have no children. My sister's gone, too, so I don't have any family left either."

How sad to be so alone in the world. "I was wondering if we could ask you a few questions about the Steadman boys."

Her forehead creased with wrinkles. "Steadman. Let's see, Peter and Len, correct?"

I shook my head. "Paul and Ben. You worked for their physician for several years. Doctor Barrows, wasn't it?"

Her face lit up at the mention of the name. "Oh my, yes. He was a wonderful man. I stayed with him for over twenty years. When he retired, I found a job at Burbank Hospital. It was all right but nothing like working for a doctor in private practice. The doctors these days though—"

She prattled on, and I didn't have the heart to interrupt her.

Restless, Jacques shifted in his seat as she continued to speak about Doctor Barrows' widow and his children. Poor thing. She probably didn't get many—if any—visitors. I hoped Jacques would not let his impatience get the best of him.

He held up his hand. "Miss Reynolds, the Steadman boys had been coming to Doctor Barrows since they were little, correct?"

She nodded. "Oh, yes. He delivered both boys. What a lovely family. Terrible shame what happened to the younger child. Why, that Pete was just the nicest boy."

I winced. "*Paul.* Um, do you remember when he started volunteering at the hospital, a few weeks before he died?"

"Such a nice boy." Then she peered at me closely through her bifocals. "You look familiar. Were you his girlfriend?"

"No, but I was a friend of his," I said. "Sometimes I'd stop by the hospital when he was working there on weekends. We'd grab lunch together."

She gave me a somber look. "That must be why you seem familiar. I'm so much better with faces instead of names. You must miss him, dear."

I swallowed hard. "Yes, I do. What type of job did you have at the hospital back then?"

Well, I worked in the emergency room," she said. "I was actually on duty the day Pete—err, Paul—was brought in. Right after he killed himself." She clucked her tongue against the roof of her mouth in dismay. "Such a waste. Terrible tragedy. And we'd been having such a nice chat the day before, too."

Jacques leaned forward eagerly. "Was he upset about something, Miss Reynolds?"

"Call me Mildred, dear." She smiled at him. "My, if I was only a few years younger." She winked at him.

Jacques smiled politely at her, but his face flushed crimson. I bit into my lower lip to keep from laughing.

"It's so hard for me to remember certain things lately. Don't ever get old, dear." She reached over to pat my hand. Her hand was fragile looking, with plentiful blue veins, and it was similar to touching an ice cube. "Let me think. We had a nice talk the day before he died. What was it he wanted to know? Oh, yes. It was odd. He was asking me questions about sterility in men." She leaned forward. "I think he might have had a little problem in that department, if you know what I mean."

I tried hard not to roll my eyes. "Did he mention if he was involved with someone?"

She blinked. "Well, dear, if he had a problem of that nature, I'm almost sure of it."

Good grief, this was embarrassing. "Did you ever see him with a woman? Besides me, that is?"

"Oh, goodness, I don't know," she laughed. "Earlier that day, a young lady was looking for him. Blonde hair, very pretty. He had just gone home, and she seemed upset to have missed him. I assumed it was his girlfriend. She'd been around a couple of times."

My heart thumped inside my chest. The description fit Rachel Kennedy. She was next on my list to visit.

"Why would he be asking about male...um, problems?"

"If I remember correctly, he had the mumps as a child," Mildred said. "That can lead to sterility in men."

"I don't remember him having the mumps."

"He may have had them as a baby, dear."

Jacques cleared his throat, obviously uncomfortable with the choice of topic. "You said you were there when they brought his body in?"

Mildred sighed. "Oh my, yes. What a terrible day. He had a faint heartbeat, so they thought maybe there was a chance but sadly, no. He died minutes afterward. I was holding his hand at the time." She frowned and gazed off into the distance. "What was it about his hand?"

Jacques and I glanced at each other. I was certain Mildred was talking to herself, so I placed a hand on her arm, hoping to divert her attention back to us. "Was there something else you remembered, Mildred?"

She shut her eyes. "Oh, dear. He had a small piece of paper clutched in his hand. But there was something that struck me as odd about it…"

I tried to control my excitement. Maybe this was the answer I was looking for. "Take your time. As long as you need. Do you think it was a suicide note?"

She shook her head, clearly frustrated. "No, because I would have turned that over to the police. The other nurse on duty was new, young, and terribly impatient. Not fit for the job, if you ask me. Anyway, she threw it away when I was out of the room. But I remember that it struck me as odd, though. There was a name on it, I believe."

"Whose name?" I asked.

She blinked rapidly. "Sorry, dear. I get tired so easily these days. I should go lie down. Maybe it will come to me later."

Although disappointed, I figured there was probably nothing I could say that would jar her memory right now. Jacques and I both stood to leave.

I handed Mildred my business card. "Thank you so much for your time. Please call me if you happen to remember anything else. You can phone me any time of day or night. This is very important."

Her sharp eyes observed me in a thoughtful manner. "You never said why you wanted the information, dear."

There was no reason for me not tell her the truth, and I hoped that maybe the admission might help stimulate her memory further. "I don't believe Paul committed suicide. I think he was murdered."

Mildred gave a small gasp and covered her mouth with both of her hands. "Oh my goodness. Of course I'll let you know if I remember anything."

We said our good-byes and let ourselves out. As I shut the

front door, I noticed Mildred was staring at the floor, transfixed, hands gripping the sides of her wheelchair. Guilt overcame me. I hadn't wanted to scare the poor woman. But I needed answers and prayed that she could provide some.

Jacques and I made a quick stop at a nearby Starbucks where I wisely ordered an herbal tea instead of my usual coffee, hoping it would help settle my stomach. As we were getting back in his convertible, my phone buzzed. I looked down at the name on the screen and shrieked. "It's Tricia!"

Jacques' coffee cup went flying out of his hand and across the parking lot. He started waving his arms frantically. "Don't keep her waiting. But play it cool! And for God's sake, don't sound desperate!"

I'd never seen my friend in such a state before, but I understood his frenzy. If one thing was certain, we were both desperate for this sale. The sooner we could sell this place, the better and in more ways than one.

I placed my hand at my throat to steady myself. "Hello, this is Cindy. How may I assist you?"

"Cindy, dear," Tricia cooed into the phone. "I have an offer on the Steadman place. I'd like for you and Jacques to present it to Mr. and Mrs. Steadman. Today, if possible."

I glanced up to see Jacques standing there with his hands clasped together, eyes pleading. If the situation hadn't been so dire, I might have laughed out loud. "Of course, Tricia. We'll swing by your office in a few minutes to pick the offer up."

Jacques pumped his fist in the direction of the sky.

"Wonderful. I look forward to seeing you." She disconnected.

I smiled at my friend. "I guess I'd better call Ben and tell him we have an offer."

"Yesss!" Jacques grabbed me around the waist and lifted me off of my feet into the air, swinging me around.

"Put me down! I'm getting dizzy."

He released me and kissed the top of my head. "I feel like break dancing right here in the parking lot."

I laughed as I got into the passenger seat. "Come on. I told her we'd be right there. And I'll call Ben and Michelle to see if we can swing by afterward."

Jacques zoomed off like a maniac while I clutched the door handle for support. He pointed at the phone in my hand. "Call Ariel Jones. She was in the office earlier. Ask her if she can take my four o'clock showing. There're copies of the paperwork on my desk in a file labeled Carter."

I made the two calls and hit pay dirt with both. Ariel was just getting ready to leave the office and gladly agreed to fill in for Jacques. Ben was at work but assured me he'd phone Michelle, and they could meet us at the house in about half an hour.

"Hey, my stomach's in knots as it is. Please slow down unless you want me to decorate your upholstery."

He turned his head and frowned. "Don't even joke about such a thing, darling. Do you have any idea what this car cost me?"

The convertible came to a screeching halt in front of Tricia's office, and Jacques stared at me with concern. "You still don't look well."

I leaned my head against the passenger side window. "I am feeling better though. Do you want me to go in?"

"Nah. She loves me. I'll grab the paperwork and be right back. You rest, dear."

Sighing, I took a sip of tea and settled back in the seat. My phone buzzed again. I stared down at the screen but didn't recognize the number.

"This is Cindy. How may I assist you?"

"Cindy, it's Aaron Connors. I was wondering if you'd gone to see that woman yet."

"Hi, Aaron. Thank you so much for all the help. I'm going to try to meet with Rachel tomorrow or maybe even tonight."

He coughed into the phone. "Just be careful. Like I said, the woman has some priors. Apparently she was stalking a woman who dated a former boyfriend of hers. Sounds like she's still up to her old tricks, even after twenty-five years."

"I'll take Jacques along, if I can convince Rachel to see me, that is. I just spoke with the nurse who was on duty that day at the hospital when Paul's body—" I paused for a moment, as the image of that day once again filled my head. "She was working in the emergency room and said he had a faint heartbeat. Then she commented that there was something strange about Paul's hand. He was holding a piece of paper."

There was a pause before Aaron spoke. "That seems highly unlikely. We would have taken it for evidence."

"Mildred said that it was clutched tightly inside, so perhaps you never saw it. She said it wasn't a suicide note or anything like that. And she said the other nurse threw it away when she was out of the room."

Aaron swore and then apologized. "I never saw a case where so many details got botched up like that one. It's downright embarrassing. Back then, we didn't have DNA to focus on like now. Too bad there's not an item of the kid's clothing or anything else from that day still around. Evidence like that would be instrumental in tracking down a potential killer."

I nodded absently, half listening to what he was saying, still thinking about what could have been in Paul's hand. Then his words dawned on me. "Oh my God."

"What is it?"

Jacques approached the car triumphantly, waving the folder Tricia had given him. I held a finger up to my lips. "I have his hat."

"Come again?"

Excitedly, I clutched the phone closer. "He was wearing a New York Mets hat the day he died. His brother gave it to me the other day as a keepsake. Their mother had kept it locked away in the attic for years, and Ben just stumbled across it a few weeks ago. It's still in a plastic bag. I don't think anyone has even opened it since that...day."

Jacques watched me, his mouth hanging open as the words registered with him.

"Damn." Aaron breathed heavily on the other end of the line. "If that's true, it looks like you might have found yourself a valuable piece of evidence."

Now both my heart and my stomach were doing flip flops. "Could that tell us who killed Paul?"

"It's a little more complicated than that," he said. "If they find DNA on the hat, they might be able to match it with the person you believe shot him. If this person has any type of record on file, that is. Are you sure the hat's never been touched?"

"I'm not positive but think there's a good chance." Was there some way I could ask Ben? No, better not to tell him anything. "The hat is at my house. Is there any way you could help us get it tested?"

Aaron was silent on the other end of the line. "I have a friend in the lab who owes me a favor. I don't really like to ask for things like this, but as I told you the other day, this case and the numerous screw-ups have always bothered me. I'd like to learn the truth, as much as you."

I doubted anyone wanted to know the answer as much as I did but didn't argue. The need to learn what had really happened was consuming to the point where it had started to gnaw at me. "Then you'll help me?"

"Drop it off at my house tonight."

Yes. "Jacques and I will drive it over within a couple of hours." I put my hand over the phone and whispered to my friend. "Is that okay?"

Jacques nodded. "I'm at your disposal for the entire evening, dear."

"Whenever you get here is fine," Aaron said. "I'll be home all evening and will run it to the lab first thing tomorrow morning. Of course, it depends on what else they have going on, but I'm betting they can get it back to me by Friday."

I was amazed. "So fast?"

Aaron chuckled. "Like I said, he owes me a favor. And a big one too. We always take care of our own, little lady." With that, he disconnected.

Jacques pulled up into the sprawling driveway of the Steadman mansion, placed the car in park, and turned to face me. "So what's the plan, Hastings?"

I grinned. "Think we might have time for a visit to see Rachel Kennedy tonight?"

He smiled. "I told you I'm at your disposal. Do you think we should call first or just show up?"

"Let's take our chances and show up."

Jacques nodded in approval. "I think that's a good idea. I mean, why would psycho chick want to talk to you, of all people? She knows you and Paul were best friends, right?"

I placed the phone back in my purse. "Everyone knew we were friends."

"Well, there you go. Bet she was jealous of you."

I pushed the car door open. "That's crazy. There was nothing even going on between the two of us."

He winked. "Well, maybe nothing on your end, darling, but I believe Paul would have disagreed with you."

I shut my car door. "You don't quit, do you?"

"Okay. Let's keep our heads in the game now. No mention of Paul's death. Our only goal for the present is to get them to accept this offer."

I put out my hand for the folder. "I didn't even look at the price yet."

"Believe it or not, it's better than I expected from Tricia. That woman lowballs everyone." Jacques handed the folder over and then glanced at my face. "Your color is improving. How's the stomach doing?"

"I'm fine. The tea helped a lot. And if Michelle and Ben agree to this offer, I have a feeling that I'll want to do some break dancing too."

CHAPTER TWELVE

*B*en answered the front door himself. He was dressed in his usual suit, this time a light gray one with matching silk tie and a gray-and-white striped oxford. "Cindy, Jacques. What perfect timing. I just got home. Please come in."

I handed him the shopping bag full of clothes that Michelle had bought for Darcy. "This is for Michelle. Darcy phoned her earlier, and she's expecting it."

He glanced at the bag, momentarily confused, and then passed it to Wesley, who was now standing beside him. "Please take these upstairs. Don't disturb Mrs. Steadman, though."

Wesley nodded. "Will you be wanting coffee, sir?"

Ben looked at us, and we both shook our heads. "No, we're fine, Wesley, thank you," he said.

The man nodded and ascended the stairs with the shopping bag.

"Let's go out on the terrace." Ben removed his jacket and placed it on a chair. "There's a nice breeze, and I could use the air after being tied up in my stuffy office all day."

He led the way outside, and we followed. I prayed Ben

couldn't hear my stomach rumbling, this time from nerves. "Won't Michelle be joining us?"

Ben waited until we had been seated and then nodded toward the second-floor window that I knew was their bedroom. "Michelle's not feeling well. Migraine. She gets them frequently and asked that I apologize to the both of you. She's fine with me making the decision. I know her thoughts on the subject and how eager she is to move. I'll show her the contract later when she's feeling better. If necessary, I can sign for her as well."

I had to secretly wonder if Michelle didn't want to face me after I had forced Darcy to phone her earlier and say that she would be returning the clothes. After Darcy had mumbled a quick good-bye to Michelle, she'd turned on me with her usual venomous "I hate you" response and had flown upstairs. This was becoming a daily thing. I had wanted to have a few moments alone with Michelle, but since I didn't want to jeopardize the sale, maybe this was just as well.

Ben glanced at the folder in Jacques' hand with curiosity. "I have to say, I'm very impressed. The house has only been on the market for three days."

Jacques flushed with pride. "It doesn't always happen this fast, believe me. But your house was priced to sell, and even in this dismal market, there are people looking in your price range. Tricia Hudson from Primer Properties has an out-of-town client who wanted exactly what your house had to offer."

Jacques opened the folder, and Ben glanced through the contract Tricia had drawn up, more specifically, at the bottom-line figure her buyers were offering.

"I know it's fifty grand less than what you were looking for," Jacques said. "We can always refuse or make a counteroffer."

Ben smiled. "Nope, we're good." He signed his name with a flourish on the line above where it had been printed.

Jacques and I looked at each other, dumbfounded. Why

weren't all of them this easy? My first ever million-dollar sale was going off without a hitch. In the past, I'd had deals for a fraction of this cost that had been nothing but constant headaches. I pinched my upper arm. Was I dreaming?

"Excellent," Jacques said.

I managed to hide my smile as I stared at my best friend. He was suave, smooth, and unruffled. This was not the same man who had done a somersault in the Starbucks parking lot about a half an hour ago.

Jacques cleared his throat. "The only stipulation is that the Whitakers would like to take possession as soon as possible. Since they're paying cash, that does away with the need for a mortgage and the holdup we'd likely encounter with the bank. They'd prefer to have inspections completed on Friday, if that's okay with you. And they'd like to be settled here within two weeks. I know it's an awful short time frame, but that's when Mr. Whitaker's movie is scheduled to start filming in the area."

Ben nodded his approval. "That works for us. To tell you the truth, I'm going out of town on business tomorrow. My last trip, I hope. I may still need to make another one once we're settled in Bermuda. Michelle has already been in touch with a moving company about packing everything for us. She may even be able to get them over here in the next couple of days, so that's not an issue. I doubt two weeks will be a problem."

He was silent for a moment as he gazed off beyond the pool. "I'd just as soon not come back here at all. When my business trip is over, I'm thinking I might fly directly to Bermuda. Michelle can arrange to meet me whenever she finishes up here. I'm assuming you two could take care of everything at the closing for us, as long as we've signed the papers in advance?"

A small twinge of doubt pecked at my brain. This was all *too* easy. Something *had* to go wrong. In desperation, I tried to shake off my glass-is-half-empty attitude, but that wasn't an easy thing. When it came to my real estate career, something *always* went wrong. I managed to force a smile to my lips. "Of course, Ben. We can take care of everything for you."

He sighed. "I'm very grateful to you both. In all honesty, Michelle and I should have left here a long time ago. I never really wanted to live in this house after what happened to Paul. Now that there may be a different conclusion, I think it's best that we move away as soon as possible."

I nodded. "I certainly understand your feelings."

Ben pinched the bridge of his nose between his forefinger and thumb while I examined his face. He looked tired. I was curious if his eagerness to move away had something to do with the former young intern in his office, but didn't dare ask.

Ben's gaze met mine. "Have you found out anything of interest concerning Paul?"

I exchanged glances with Jacques, who stared back at me in return, his green eyes cat-like. I read the unspoken message in them. *Keep your mouth shut until the sale is final.*

I chose to ignore the warning. "Was Paul carrying on with anyone when he died?"

He looked thunderstruck. "Why would you ask that, especially after the note he left you?"

I really didn't want to get into the delicate subject of Paul's conversation with Mildred. Jacques nudged me under the table, but I ignored him. I wasn't sure what Rachel might tell us later —if anything—and I hoped Ben could provide some useful facts about his brother. "Do you remember Mildred Reynolds?"

His expression was blank. "The name sounds familiar."

"She was a nurse for Doctor Barrows."

"Oh!" He nodded. "I do remember her. Nice lady. Is she still around?"

"Yes, we drove out to visit her earlier. She's confined to a wheelchair, and her mind is starting to decline a bit. But she said that Paul had come to her the day before his death. He had some concerns about—um, about male sterility."

He looked at me like I had corn growing out of my ears. "Why in God's name would he have asked her about such a thing?"

"That's what I'd like to know," I said. "I hoped you might be able to shed some light on this."

He shook his head. "You know that we weren't close. As far as I know, there weren't any girls he was interested in—besides you, of course. So this really doesn't make sense. Perhaps the woman is confusing him with a patient. Did she say anything else?"

I debated briefly about how much more to tell him, but I also wanted to gauge his reaction. "She was in the emergency room the day Paul died and said he was holding something odd in his hand."

Ben's dark eyes were huge in his pale face. "What was it?"

"She couldn't remember."

He loosened his tie and made a face. "If we'd had a decent police department back then, things could have gone differently. How are we ever going to get any answers now?"

I bit into my lower lip. "I'm not going to give up until I *do* have answers."

Ben smiled. "You were a good, loyal friend to him, Cindy. Maybe if Paul had lived, you would have been my sister-in-law."

Embarrassment flooded my body. "I-I don't know about that. I loved your brother, but I wasn't *in love* with him."

"Yeah, I know something about that too."

He spoke so low that, for a moment, I wasn't sure I'd heard him correctly. Then a shadow passed over his face. "You might think you're incapable of loving someone, but it's always possible. So there's never any way to be sure."

Was he talking about me or himself? I caught Jacques raising his eyebrows at me in warning and guessed what he was thinking. He was concerned that something would end up costing us this sale. I wasn't about to let that happen.

"I'm hoping that Mildred might remember whatever was in Paul's hand. I have a feeling that might hold the key to everything."

"If I could go back and do things differently, I would. We were never close, but Paul was my only sibling, and I did love him in my own way. To think that someone was in this house that day and might have taken his life—" Ben blew out a sharp breath. "This is all very difficult for me to fathom. Have you found out anything else?"

Jacques kicked me under the table again. I was confident my leg was black and blue by this time. "No. I seem to have hit a dead end."

Something flickered in his eyes that made me think he didn't believe me. A chill ran down my spine.

Jacques rose to his feet. "Well, we won't keep you. Please give our regards to Michelle. Cindy will be in touch and let you know what time the inspections are scheduled for when she hears from Tricia."

Ben nodded. "You'll be present for the inspections, correct?"

Jacques smiled. "If possible, we will both be here."

I deftly raised one eyebrow at him, but he ignored the gesture. *Sheesh.* Didn't he think I was capable of handling anything by myself? Yet, I couldn't blame Jacques. I hadn't exactly been Miss Dependable lately.

Ben walked us to the front door. "I guess this is good-bye then." He shook hands with Jacques. When I extended mine he ignored it, pulling me forward into a tight hug instead. "Please share anything you find out about Paul's death with me. I want to know every detail."

I stared over his shoulder into Jacques' bewildered face. "Of course."

Ben released me, and for a moment, I thought he was going to say something else. He must have thought better of it because he opened the door and waited until we had walked down the driveway and were situated in Jacques car. He waved one last time and shut the front door.

Jacques said nothing as he started the engine and turned around in the driveway. As soon as we reached the road, I couldn't stand it anymore. "Okay. You're ticked at me."

"Gee, whatever gave you that idea?"

I blew out a breath. "I'm not trying to jeopardize the sale, honest. It's just that—well…"

Jacques' convertible skidded to a stop as he pulled the car over to the side of the road. He grabbed me by the shoulders and turned around me to face him, his eyes an emerald inferno. "The hell with the stupid house. I'm worried about you. Why did you tell Ben about what Mildred said? He could have been the one who shot Paul, for all you know. Cynthia, you could be getting yourself in deep doo-doo here. I don't want anything to happen to you."

My eyes started to fill as I reached out to hug my friend. "I'm going to be fine. Jeez, I don't know what to say. I was sure you were upset about the sale."

"I can always find another mansion for sale," he said gruffly, "but I can't find another you."

Tears dripped off my chin in an unladylike manner. Jacques sighed as he reached into his pocket and offered me his handkerchief, which I gratefully took. "You're the one person I know who never has a tissue during a moment of crisis."

"Another reason I can't do without you." I spoke in a husky voice.

Jacques' eyes were starting to fill as well, and he immediately changed the subject. "Likewise. But I'm not convinced Ben is innocent, Cin."

"I thought he might have some idea of what had been going on with Paul. Jacques, it just doesn't make sense. Why would Paul be asking questions about sterility? Was he asking for himself or someone else?"

Jacques put the car back in drive and took a left on to the main road. "Mildred had a stroke. She's obviously having some memory issues as a result. Ben could be right. Maybe she has Paul confused with someone else."

"But she seemed to remember him well enough." Except for his name, that is. I covered my eyes with my hand. "I just feel like I'm running in circles here."

Jacques was silent until he pulled the convertible into the driveway behind my Honda. I stared at my watch. Five-thirty. Where the heck had the day gone? "Let me just change my clothes and pop the casserole I made last night into the oven, and then I'll be ready to roll."

"Where does this stalker, Rachel, live?" Jacques asked.

"Believe it or not, she's just around the corner from Lambert Court—you know—where Aaron lives. An apartment complex on Summer Drive."

His lips curled back in distaste. "I know that place. It's a dive. This is going to be so much fun."

I ignored the sarcasm dripping from his mouth as we opened our car doors in unison. I shut mine and heard a shriek. Stevie and Seth came running in our direction.

"Hi, Uncle Jacques! What did you bring me?" Stevie looked as if he'd just been rolling around in the mud. As he ran toward Jacques, my friend's face and body both froze with fear.

I ran in Stevie's direction, cutting him off. "Stop! Don't you dare mess up Uncle Jacques' suit."

I managed to grab Stevie just in the nick of time. Jacques remained standing in place, a deer-in-the-headlights look plastered on his face. He stared from Stevie to Seth, who was also covered in dirt, then shook his head and grinned. "You guys been working construction again?"

That got a giggle out of them. Jacques reached into his coat pocket and produced a pack of gum. "Sorry, guys. I didn't know

I was coming here, otherwise I would have been more prepared."

"That's okay." Seth grabbed the gum and then reached for Jacques' hand, leading him toward the house. "You can make it up to us next time."

We all trooped inside.

"You guys get upstairs and take a shower," I said. "And be quick about it. Dinner will be ready soon."

Greg was in the study but came out when he heard me speak. He smiled at Jacques and then placed his arms around my waist and kissed me. "I was starting to wonder where you were. Everything okay?"

"Just fine, honey."

He pumped Jacques hand. "Why don't you join us for dinner? Cindy always makes more than enough."

Jacques shook his head. "Thanks, but Ed's bringing me something from the restaurant later—after we get back, that is."

The smile left Greg's face as he stared at both of us. "You mean you're going out again? Is there another showing?"

"Uncle Jacques," Stevie yelled from the top of the stairs. "Seth's in the shower, so come on up, and see the new Lego set we got. You can even build a mansion with this one."

"Hmm. That sounds right up my alley." Jacques winked at me. "Yell when you're ready to go, dear."

I went into the kitchen and turned the oven on, then grabbed the casserole from the fridge that I had prepared last night. "It just needs to cook for half an hour," I said to Greg. "Then it will be ready to go."

Greg didn't answer. I turned around to see him watching me, a stern expression on his handsome face, arms folded across his broad chest. "I want to know how your doctor's appointment went. And don't give me that 'I'm fine' bit because I know you're keeping something from me."

I shut the oven door. "I don't have the results yet. Honest.

But there's a chance it might not be menopause—I may have an ulcer instead."

He frowned. "And from the lilt in your voice, that's good news?"

"Of course it's good news. Who wants to go through the change?"

Greg sighed as he drew me toward him and smoothed back the hair from my face. "Where are you and Jacques really going tonight? Does this have something to do with Paul?"

I stared at the concern in his ocean-blue eyes. "We're going to see a woman I went to high school with. She had a huge crush on Paul and used to follow him around like a puppy dog back then." Okay, it was more like a rottweiler, but there was no need to get into specifics now, right?

He caressed my cheek with his fingers. "I don't like you playing detective. Remember what happened the last time? You almost got yourself killed. And with a possible health issue, you should be taking it easy now."

I was touched by his concern. "I'm fine, honest. And when I get the results from the doctor and know what's going on, I'll be even better. Maybe this is just a mind-over-matter thing."

"Do you really think so?"

"Sure," I lied. "We won't be gone long. Rachel may not even be home. But I have to try. I'm positive my gut instinct is right about this, Greg."

Greg ran a hand through his hair, clearly frustrated. "All right, sweetheart. Maybe it will finally give you some peace of mind if you can get to the bottom of this."

That was my hope, too. "I need to go upstairs and change."

He grinned at me in a teasing manner. "Need any help?"

"Sheesh, you're in overdrive twenty-four hours a day lately."

He put his arms around my waist again. "It's your fault for being so gorgeous."

I laughed and tried to wriggle out of his grasp. "Where's Darcy?"

Greg released his hold on me. "She went over to Heather's. I told her to be back at six o'clock for dinner."

"She's still upset with me."

"Forget about it. You did the right thing. And she knew better than to take those clothes in the first place. Once you sell that house, Michelle will move away, and things will get back to normal again around here."

I'd forgotten about that part. Another score for me. "Speaking of which, we got an offer on their place today. Ben just signed the contract."

Greg's mouth fell open in surprise. "Wow, that's fantastic. But it only went on the market the other day. It hasn't even been a full week yet."

I shrugged. "Sometimes it just works out like that."

"Hmm." He scratched his head thoughtfully. "But it never works out like that for *you*, Cin."

Sadly, he was right.

CHAPTER THIRTEEN

*I*t was past seven when Jacques pulled his car up in front of the three-story, dilapidated apartment building that Rachel Kennedy resided in. The gray paint was peeling off the sides, windows were filthy, and the asphalt roof looked as if it was about ready to cave in.

Jacques came around and opened the car door for me. "La dump awaits you, mademoiselle."

"Hilarious."

We'd already dropped the hat off to Aaron, who'd promised to take it to his friend at the lab first thing in the morning. I said I'd call him on Friday if he didn't get in touch with me first. We'd exchanged a few pleasantries before Jacques and I sped off again.

"What floor is she on?" Jacques asked.

I checked my Post-It Note. "Second. Apartment 2B."

We climbed a flight of rickety stairs that I worried might collapse underneath us at any second. As we reached the darkened second floor, I gagged and covered my mouth and nose, afraid I might be sick. Someone was cooking with garlic and herbs, and the smell was detrimental to my already-sensitive stomach. I prayed the concoction wasn't coming from Rachel's apartment.

Jacques raised his hand to knock on the battered door, then stopped for a moment to read the profanity on the wall with interest. Someone had written a four-letter word in large, block lettering, and underneath it was another thought provoking comment about one's mother.

He grabbed a handkerchief from his pocket and covered the doorknob with it. "God knows what you might catch around this place. And I'm half expecting someone to come running toward us with a knife at any moment. Maybe they filmed *Psycho* here."

As the words left his mouth, the door was yanked open, and a slim woman with cropped blonde hair stared out at us. One look told me it was Rachel. She stared at Jacques, puzzled, and then her gaze came to rest on me.

"I know you," she said. "Aren't you a cop?"

This was a first. "No. We went to high school together. My name is—was—Cindy Haskins."

She took a long drag of her cigarette and blew it directly into my face. I turned away, coughing and sputtering.

"Yeah. I remember now. So why are you here?"

Jacques' eyes glittered at her. "That was totally uncalled for. Cindy isn't feeling well, and you aren't helping matters."

"And...I'm supposed to care...why?"

I tried to keep the peace, fearful she wouldn't let us in. "This is my friend and business associate, Jacques Forte. We were hoping we could talk to you for a minute."

Her eyes crossed back to Jacques and took in the expensive suit and Rolex he was wearing, the latter a wedding present from Ed. "Well, color me happy. Looks like it's my lucky day." She slammed the door against the wall and then walked back inside. We interpreted that as our invitation to enter.

The place was almost barren of furniture. There was a small

kitchen with dirty dishes stacked in the sink and several pizza boxes on the counter. An open partition separated the room from the combination dining and living area. A small sofa, television, metal table, and two chairs were the only furniture present. The once-white walls were dingy from smoke, and there was a series of holes in the Sheetrock. The laminate flooring was broken in several places.

Since we were not offered a seat, we remained standing as Rachel plopped herself down on the sofa. I studied her face while she stubbed her cigarette out into a glass ashtray. The prettiness and birdlike qualities I'd remembered from high school were long gone. Her crystal-blue eyes that had once been so alive and fresh had dulled. Her face was compounded with a brittle, sullen look. I wondered how difficult her life had been and if drugs had played a part as well.

Rachel's figure was still excellent. She wore a pair of skinny jeans and a white tank top. She was well endowed, and it was painfully obvious she hadn't bothered to don a bra either. Jacques' face turned crimson, and he tried to look elsewhere.

"How come you weren't at the reunion the other night?" I asked.

She lit another cigarette with a match from her jeans pocket and stared at me for a moment, then burst into peals of laughter. "Is that why you're here?"

"Sort of," I said.

"Why would old Benny boy want me at his house? He always looked down on me like I was some type of vermin."

"Was that because you ran after his brother?" Jacques asked.

She opened her mouth in surprise. "What is this? Are you reporters for the Alumni Annual or something?"

I ignored her sarcasm. "Why don't you think Ben liked you?"

"Oh, please. I may have been a cheerleader, but I didn't exactly run with the rest of the rich and beautiful crowd. My parents didn't have two nickels to rub together. I had to work a part-time job on weekends just so I could afford the uniforms. But you—you wouldn't understand about that."

"Excuse me." I spoke calmly. "I *do* happen to understand. It was just me and my mother. We didn't have any money either. You're not the only one who worked a job while in school. And my money didn't go toward uniforms. It went to help my mother pay the rent for our apartment."

"Yeah, but I'm sure Paulie took good care of you." Her eyes glittered as they came to rest on my face.

I counted to five before answering. "Paul and I were friends. That's all."

She snorted. "Sure you were. You really expect me to believe you two weren't fooling around?"

Anger formed in a ball at the pit of my stomach and crept upwards until I tasted bile in the back of my throat. I was so tired of trying to defend my friendship with Paul to other people. "I really don't care what you believe. Now, let's hear what you know about his death."

Rachel's face was shell shocked. "What the hell is that supposed to mean? He killed himself."

I placed my hands on my hips and thrust my chest forward. "No, he didn't."

She watched me with interest. "After all these years? How do you know? What proof do you even have?"

Jacques shot me a look of warning, but I shook my head at him. "The proof is none of your business. I happen to know his death was not a result of suicide." I took a deep breath and continued. "And I think you had something to do with it."

Her nostrils flared as she rose to her feet and walked toward me, placing her face right next to mine. Her breath reeked of beer and tobacco, but I didn't back down.

"How dare you," she said, the spittle from her mouth hitting my cheek.

I raised a hand to wipe my face, but my gaze didn't waver.

"You used to stalk him all the time. Maybe you figured if you couldn't have him, no one else should."

She took a step back and sucked on her cigarette again, watching the billows of smoke move through the air. "I was crazy about Paul, yeah, but I never would have hurt him."

"You were already hurting him. You didn't let the poor guy breathe. Every step he took, you were there, watching him."

"A few years earlier and she could have been an inspiration for The Police's song," Jacques mumbled.

Rachel shot him a dirty look and stubbed out her second cigarette. She started to reach for another and then decided against it. Her eyes locked onto mine. "Paul Steadman never gave me the time of day. And I wasn't the only one chasing after him, believe me."

Here we go again. "*I* didn't chase after him. We were friends. Best friends, in fact."

Rachel gave an exaggerated snort. "I wasn't referring to you, sweetie. There were plenty of girls hot for Paulie. Especially my fellow cheerleaders. He didn't play football, but he was pretty easy on the eyes, smart, *and* he was rich, which didn't exactly hurt his case."

I clenched my fists at my sides. I hated hearing her describe Paul in such a callous manner.

Jacques shifted his weight and leaned against the wall. "So you weren't carrying on with him? Never even had a one-night stand?"

"Hell, I wish. He was always polite to me, but it was obvious he wasn't interested. I hoped he would change his mind after a while." She lifted her bottle of Budweiser from the floor and took a long sip. "But he did have other conquests."

"Who?" I asked. "Who was he fooling around with?"

Rachel folded her arms over her chest. "What's it worth to you?"

Jacques clamped his lips together in a fine, thin line. "Don't waste your time on this one, Cynthia. She's lying. It's obvious she's only looking for a payout. Come on. Let's go."

I was torn. "If you really cared about him, then you'd tell me. Don't you want to see him get justice?"

She snorted. "Who cares about justice for him? He's already dead. What about justice for me?"

I couldn't stand it anymore. "What exactly is your problem? You seem to feel like the world is responsible for the condition your life is in."

Her eyes blazed with hatred. "Don't you dare talk about *my* life. You know nothing about me. Go back to your husband, kiddies, and your nice ranch in the suburbs, and leave me alone. Got it?"

"Fine." I nodded to Jacques. "Let's go."

As we turned toward the door, she gave a low, cackling laugh. "You're just another one like Michelle Steadman."

That stopped me cold. "What have you got against Michelle? You were good friends in high school."

Rachel shrugged. "Michelle was a user. Still is, I bet. She started out like me. Born with a plastic spoon in her mouth but wanted silver. Hey, at least *she* got what she wanted. That's where any similarities ended for us. She has everything she could ever want out of life. Rich, good-looking husband and a beautiful daughter. Me, I've got nothing. Zilch. A worthless user of a man who knocked me around and stole my money to support his habit. My kids are grown now and won't even talk to me."

My anger started to turn to pity, but she prattled on before I could add anything to the conversation.

"I mean...how many of us can say we slept with *both* of the Steadman brothers?"

My hand was on the doorknob as her words registered with me. It was insane, ludicrous. My legs started to shake while I whirled around to face her. "Are you saying that Paul slept with Michelle?"

She giggled. "Kind of changes the way you feel about him, huh?"

I spotted Jacques watching me out of the corner of my eye, his face full of concern. "I will *never* believe that. I think you're just saying that because you're jealous of Michelle."

Rachel gave me a pointed look. "Believe what you want. I saw them leaving the hospital together the day before he died. I'd come by to invite him to a party. The girl at the desk lied and told me he wasn't there. But then I spotted them talking in the parking lot. They looked pretty chummy too. You figure the rest out."

I exchanged glances with Jacques. A sickening feeling similar to dread descended over me. *Was it really possible? No.* I couldn't imagine Paul would hurt his brother like that. But why else would they have been together? Doctor Sanchez had said he spotted him with a blonde woman the day before, and they'd been arguing. I'd assumed it was Rachel. Had I been wrong?

"Did you have an argument with Paul the day before he died?"

She ignored my question and stretched her arms out over the back of the couch, watching me with curiosity. "Yep, Michelle knew how to get around. And before Ben and Paul, she kept herself busy screwing the quarterback."

"Carl Williams?"

She nodded and reached for her beer bottle again. "Yeah. Mr. Blond and Beautiful himself. Gotta hand it to her. Michelle always went for the top of the food chain. Paulie might have had a thing for you, but it didn't stop him from bedding her."

Jacques glared at her and placed a hand on my arm. "You can't trust anything that comes out of her mouth, dear. Come on, let's blow this joint."

Rachel placed the beer bottle down and wiped her mouth

with the back of her hand. "Do what you want. It still doesn't make you any better than me though."

He cast an irritated glance in her direction. "No one ever said that. Truth be known, I feel sorry for you."

"Sorry for me?" Rachel shrieked at him. "Don't you *dare* feel sorry for me. I don't want or need your pity. Now get the hell out."

Her scathing eyes focused on me again. "And as for you, bitch. You think you're so high and mighty? Yeah, right. If Paul had lived, you would have married him for his money in a heartbeat. I know your type. Love's not important. Cold, hard cash is all that counts in this world."

I sucked in some air and took a step toward her, so enraged that my vision blurred for a moment. Fortunately, Jacques grabbed my arm just in time, because I wasn't sure what would have happened if I'd reached her.

"She's not worth it," he said. "Let's go, Cin."

"Yeah, Cin," Rachel mocked me. "Here's your hat. What's your hurry? Now get out of here." She gave me the finger.

Jacques pursed his lips. "My, such a lady."

She leaned back against the couch and belched. "I know. I try not to put on airs, but it's hard sometimes."

My phone buzzed in my purse, but I chose to ignore it. I couldn't figure this woman out. She obviously hated her life and wanted everyone to be as miserable as she was. Could I trust anything that came out of her mouth? Doubtful.

I was really pushing the envelope but no longer cared. "You can say what you want, but you never loved Paul. And I happen to know that you were arrested for stalking someone else recently."

Rachel's face was pinched with anger. "My ex's new girl-friend. She's the reason he left me. Not that I give a damn about him anymore. He turned my kids against me."

Here goes nothing. "How do we know you didn't kill Paul in a jealous rage?"

She dismissed us with a wave of her hand. "Like I said, believe what you want. I really don't care. Just get the hell out of my house. *Now.*"

With trembling hands, I opened the door. Jacques was behind me, his hand on the small of my back in a protective gesture.

"Oh and Cindy?"

I turned around. Rachel was now standing beside the couch, beer bottle in hand. For a moment, I wondered if she planned to throw it at us. Her piercing blue eyes of steel focused on my face as her lips twisted into a manic smile.

"You really should be careful before you go around accusing people of murder. Maybe next time it won't just be the windshield of your car that gets broken."

CHAPTER FOURTEEN

"*W*ell, there's your answer," Jacques said. "Rachel knows something about Paul's death. I'd bet the Steadman mansion on it."

At Jacques' suggestion, we had stopped at Starbucks once again. He'd been grousing how badly he needed a latte after spilling his earlier in the parking lot. Not that I was complaining. I was always up for my favorite coffee chain, any time of day or night.

We were sitting in one of the booths with the welcoming smell of coffee beans and cinnamon wafting through the air. Jacques started to say something else, but I shook my head at him as I finished listening to the voicemail message on my phone.

"Who was that?"

I took a long sip of my caramel macchiato. Heaven in a cup, and by some miracle, it had also helped to settle my stomach. "Mildred Reynolds. She wants me to stop over tomorrow morning. Will you go with me?"

"Sure. What else do I have to do? I mean, it's not like I have a business to run or anything."

"There goes that sarcastic mouth of yours again." I grinned.

He smiled and then grew serious. "Why couldn't she just tell you over the phone? It's almost an hour away, even at the speed I drive. I hate to say it, Cin, but this is just another attempt to get you back over there. She's lonely and wants the company."

I knew he was right, but still, I pitied the woman. "Maybe she remembered the name on the paper. I can't afford not to check it out. And it seems like no one even cares about the poor thing. Come on, how long could it take…a couple of hours maybe? Say, why don't we bring her a macchiato and a croissant too? I bet that would make her day."

Jacques sighed. "Oh, fine. Just keep your phone nearby tomorrow because Tricia will be calling to let you know what time the inspections are scheduled for on Friday."

"I wish they could be tomorrow instead. Greg's working from home but not on Friday. I hate to ask Darcy for anything these days. She's so angry with me over the whole Michelle thing."

Jacques snorted. "Teenagers. Something I look forward to. *Not.* Okay, we'll go see Mildred first thing and get that over with. How about I pick you up at nine?"

"Sounds good."

"What's your theory so far? I'm convinced that nutcase Rachel has something to do with his death."

I spooned some whipped cream into my mouth. "I don't know. She's obviously a loose cannon, and it sounds like her life has been miserable from the get-go. I suppose it's possible Rachel could have killed Paul in a fit of passion. If she didn't do it, maybe she was an accessory."

Jacques raised his eyebrows at me. "To whom? So maybe two people were involved? And why was Paul asking the nurse questions about sterility?"

"That is really weird. But Paul was like a sponge, always absorbing knowledge. Maybe he was asking for someone else."

Jacques smiled. "Maybe he was planning on proposing to you and wanted to make sure he could have kids, because of the mumps and all."

I rolled my eyes. "He was eighteen years old and thinking about medical school. Kids were the last thing on his mind."

"But you, on the other hand, were very much on his mind, my dear."

How could I have been so blind? As I thought back now, there were signs I'd ignored. Paul wanting to slow dance at the prom and holding me extremely close. Or the time we'd gone to the beach and I'd asked him what he thought of the new bikini I'd bought. He'd looked at me with such a stupid grin I was positive he'd been making fun of me.

Jacques waved a hand in front of my face. "Are you still with me?"

"Sorry," I whispered. "I was just wondering how I'd never known."

Jacques took a sip from his latte. "Maybe you did know. Maybe you chose to block it out because you couldn't handle the truth."

I twisted a strand of hair between my fingers. "Despite how much I love Greg and adore you, I still miss having Paul in my life."

"I can understand that." He squeezed my hand. "So what do you think of Rachel's insinuation about Michelle and Paul?"

I glanced down at the table. "I may need to mention that to Michelle. With some tact, of course."

"No," Jacques said. "Not until the sale goes through."

I was astonished. "We're talking about a man's life here."

"Come on. Do you really think Paul was sleeping with Michelle? After everything you've told me about him, I'm not buying it."

Of course I didn't want to believe it either. Then I remembered Melanie's words from the other day. "Think back to when you were that age. Say that someone offered you sex with no strings attached. Would you take it? Even if you were in love with someone else?"

Jacques frowned. "My situation was a little different. At that age I was busy telling my straitlaced parents I was gay. And it didn't go over well, I assure you."

I detected bitterness in his voice. Jacques rarely talked about his childhood or his parents, who were both now deceased, but I knew they'd never come to terms with his lifestyle.

"I'm so sorry. But try to put yourself in Paul's shoes for a minute."

He sighed. "I knew several men that wouldn't have passed it up, especially from a woman as beautiful as Michelle. But from what you say, Paul didn't sound like the run of the mill guy."

I bit into my lower lip. "That's what makes this so difficult for me to understand. I can't see him sleeping with a woman who was involved with his brother. Paul had morals."

"Then back to my original assumption. Rachel's lying. Maybe she was the one Doctor Sanchez heard with Paul. You can't believe anything that comes out of that woman's mouth. She's trying to make trouble, Cin."

"Why would anyone want him dead? He was such a good guy." My voice shook slightly.

Jacques stood and crossed over to my side of the booth, extended his hand to help me out, and then kissed me on the cheek. "Come on. It's past seven-thirty. You should go home and spend some time with your man. We'll talk more about this tomorrow."

With a sigh, I walked over and threw my cup in the trash and then made my way to the door, which Jacques was holding open for me. He placed a comforting arm around my shoulders. "Go home and get some rest. As Scarlett would say, 'Tomorrow is another day.'"

We were silent on our way back to my house, and when he

pulled up in the driveway, I reached over to hug him. "You sure you don't want to come in?"

"Nah. Ed's on his way home. He's bringing me some takeout from the restaurant, and then we're going to unwind and watch a movie. I'm in the mood for something light. Maybe a chick flick."

"I thought Ed hated those."

Jacques grinned. "He's not getting a say this time. Did he sell a house for over a million today? Hmm, don't think so. I'll pick you up at nine sharp, love."

I opened the car door. "I'll be ready. Night."

I waved and watched him zoom off before I entered the house. Shrieks of laughter were coming from downstairs where Greg and the twins were watching an episode of SpongeBob. I wondered what my mother-in-law would say if she could see her son laughing at a starfish.

"Hi, Mom." Stevie and Seth were consuming popcorn at a furious rate from the couch. Rusty was sitting nearby, waiting patiently for them to drop more kernels on the floor.

Greg reached up from the recliner he was sitting in to wrap an arm around my waist and pulled me down into the chair with him. "There's my gorgeous girl. I was starting to worry."

Stevie made a face. "Yuck. No kissing, Dad."

With a grin, Greg touched his lips to mine while the twins started screaming and making obnoxious noises.

"Gross!" Stevie shouted.

Seth covered his eyes. "I'm going blind."

I laughed and struggled to my feet. "Where's Darcy?"

Greg jerked his finger toward the ceiling. "In her room."

"How did she seem earlier?" I asked.

Greg shrugged. "Fine, I guess. She didn't say much during dinner, but she had two helpings of the casserole, so I guess she's okay."

"Well, at least she's still eating my food," I said tartly. "I'm going upstairs to have a talk with her." I turned my attention back to the twins. "Were you two outside after dinner?"

"Maybe," Stevie said.

Greg yawned. "Yeah, they took Rusty for a walk."

I examined Seth's mud-splattered arms and pointed toward the stairs. "Get upstairs for another shower."

"Uh-uh," Seth said. "I don't need a shower. I smell fine."

Stevie gave him a push. "No, you don't. You stink like Rusty's poop."

The bowl of popcorn flew into the air as they started tussling. Within seconds, Rusty was barking and trying to jump between them—when he wasn't trying to devour the popcorn, that is.

"Enough!" I got down on my hands and knees and started picking up the mess.

Greg heaved himself out of the chair and pulled the twins apart. "Seth, take your shower first. Stevie will help me clean up."

"Oh, come on, man," Seth whined.

Greg gave me a slight pat on the backside. "Go on, baby. I'll take care of everything here."

Actually, I wouldn't have minded switching places with him but didn't say so. I knew Darcy was furious with me because I'd forced her to return the clothes. And the truth was, I still smarted from her words yesterday. It also hurt me that we weren't able to give her the same things that Michelle could.

I climbed the stairs to the main floor of the house and then ascended the staircase to the bedrooms on the second floor. I was about to knock on Darcy's door when I heard giggling coming from the other side. I pressed my ear to the door.

"That sounds like so much fun. And you were totally awesome to understand about the clothes. My mom is so square about most things these days."

I was frozen in place, listening to her happily chatter on. It had quickly become obvious who she was talking to. The words stung more than a slap in the face and left me just as breathless.

I heard her say something else, then raised my fist in the air and brought it down hard on the door. There was a brief silence, a murmur, and Darcy opened the door, looking as guilty as if she'd just snuck back in her window from a joyride with some friends.

Darcy glanced at me for a moment with a sullen expression, saying nothing. Then she turned on her heel and leaped onto her bed, where she began scrolling through her phone. It was like I wasn't even there.

I tried to stay calm despite the fact that, on the inside, a full-fledged storm was brewing. "I'd like to have a little chat with you."

She cut her eyes to me for a second, then she lowered her head and starting texting something on her phone.

So much for staying calm. I reached out and snatched the phone from her hands. "I'd appreciate you listening to me when I'm talking."

Darcy let out a long, exaggerated sigh. "What is it now?"

Annoyed, I stared at her. Lately, I never knew what type of mood my daughter might be in. The last couple of days her attitude had worsened, which I attributed to this newfound friendship with Michelle. I wished I'd never asked the woman for her help. "Were you just talking to Michelle on the phone?"

"Yeah, so?"

I sat down on the edge of her bed. She shifted her body so she didn't have to look at me. "Darcy, don't treat me like the enemy here. I'm your mother, and I happen to love you."

She whirled her head back around. "If you loved me so much, you'd want to see me happy."

"Of course I want to see you happy. Is this still about the clothes?"

Her lips formed in a genuine pout. "No. It's the fact that *you* were the one who asked Michelle to help me. And now that I like her, she's moving away. It's all your fault."

I hadn't been expecting this. "What exactly did Michelle tell you?"

"That their house had sold already, and she's leaving town Saturday to meet her husband in Bermuda. She may even take off on Friday if the movers get things done early enough. And it's all because of you. You never sell a house quickly, so why now?"

For a moment, I thought I might burst into laughter but managed to hold it in check. "I'm sorry, sweetheart. But you can't blame me. A couple saw the house, and it was just what they wanted. All I did was show it to them." Actually, I hadn't even done that. That had been Jacques' doing.

Darcy sniffed. "It's not fair. I finally find someone who can help me, and now she's going away."

I chose my words carefully. "You only met Michelle yesterday, Darcy. You really know nothing about her." *And boy could I tell you a few things.*

She snorted. "I knew you'd say that. You're not a cheerleader, Mother, so you'll never understand what it's like. Michelle totally gets it. We're going to get together on Friday after her inspections are over. Probably around noon."

Curiosity got the best of me. "Does she know what time the inspections are scheduled for?"

Darcy reached for the phone I still held in my hands. "Yeah, she said the other agent called and told her nine o'clock on Friday."

I clamped my lips together in annoyance. Why hadn't Tricia phoned *me*? It was my listing, and she was supposed to contact the agent in charge so I, in turn, could let my clients know. Why was everyone acting like I had nothing to do with this sale?

Darcy hesitated. "Um, if you don't mind, I'd like to call Ryan now. He just got off work."

I patted her arm and rose. "Of course. I wouldn't want to stand in your way." As I reached the door, I stole a glance back in her direction, but she was already gabbing away on the phone again and completely unaware of me. I'd secretly hoped Darcy might catch the note of sarcasm in my voice, but if she had, it was obvious she didn't care.

"BY THE WAY," Jacques said. "Tricia Hudson sent me a text late last night. The inspections are scheduled for nine tomorrow. You're free, right?"

It was past nine-thirty on Thursday morning, and we were on our way to Mildred's house. I was preoccupied trying to balance the tray of coffee and caramel macchiatos on my lap while also maintaining a grip on the door handle for dear life. Although almost perfect in every way imaginable, Jacques was a maniac when he drove, and I lived in constant fear for my life whenever I rode with him.

"Please slow down. My stomach is acting up again this morning. And why did Tricia call you and Michelle but not me? *Hello, I* am the agent on this deal."

Jacques cut his eyes to me. "You know Tricia isn't exactly your biggest fan."

I gritted my teeth. "Well, it would be nice if someone in this industry would bother to acknowledge me—just once."

He winked. "I always acknowledge you, darling. You're the foam in my cappuccino."

I burst out laughing and almost lost the cups in the process.

Jacques swerved around a car that dared to go the speed limit. "Cheer up, dear. What does it matter who Tricia called? In a couple of weeks, you're going to have one big, fat commission check and a new armchair in your office. Life is good."

He took a right onto Mildred's street, and we were suddenly

confronted by the sight of an EMT truck and a police car with flashing lights. They were parked directly in front of Mildred's house. A small crowd of people had gathered on the sidewalk.

An ice-cold chill swept through my body as I stared out at the crowd, my heart pounding furiously.

Jacques sucked in a sharp breath. He parked the convertible two houses down from Mildred's and cast a worried glance in my direction. "I'll go see what's happening. I'm sure she's fine, Cin. You stay here."

I tried to utter a thank you, but all I could do was continue to stare and manage a small whimper while Jacques made his way over to the crowd. He immediately began talking with a young woman. She started waving her arms dramatically as Jacques nodded and said something in return. After a minute, he turned and glanced back in my direction, his expression grim.

Deep down, I already knew it wasn't good news. Then, all of a sudden, the crowd separated as two EMTs moved past, carrying a body bag between them. They gently placed it in the back of their vehicle.

My heart stuttered inside my chest. *No God, please no. Not her.*

Jacques returned to the vehicle and shut the door. He reached over and loosened my grip on the tray of coffee cups. He actually had to pry my numb fingers from the sides of the cardboard. Then he took both of my ice-cold hands in his warm ones. His usual bright eyes were dulled with sadness as they found mine.

"Cindy, dear," he began slowly.

I heard myself make a tiny mewing sound. "What happened to her?"

He shut his eyes for a moment and then met my gaze again. "Mildred's aide found her early this morning. The upstairs neighbor said it looked like she'd been strangled to death."

My entire body revolted at his words. "She'd still be alive if I hadn't gone to see her."

"No, darling, you mustn't think like that," Jacques whispered.

I turned away from him, buried my head in my hands, and started to sob. What had I done?

CHAPTER FIFTEEN

*J*acques brought me back to the office. Fortunately, no one was there to witness my hot-mess status except for our receptionist, who was busy on a personal call. I couldn't stop crying. Jacques left me sitting in my office and ran downstairs to the microwave to fix me some tea.

He could say what he wanted, but I knew the truth. I was the reason that sweet, elderly woman was dead. Furiously, I wiped at my eyes and tried to focus. Who knew I'd been to see her?

I took a deep breath and racked my brain for some possible answers. Melanie knew about Mildred. And I'd opened my big mouth and blabbed to Ben that I was going there. Had anyone else known? Could someone have followed us there?

"Here we are." Jacques handed me a cup of tea and then set a can of ginger ale down on my desk.

I cupped the mug for warmth, hoping that it might somehow relieve the ice-cold chill that had settled into my bones.

"Listen to me, dear," Jacques said. "You need to stop blaming yourself."

I stared at him in disbelief. "Who should I blame, then? I put

Mildred in this position. If I hadn't gone to see her, she'd still be alive."

"You didn't put your hands around her neck and choke the life out of her," he argued. "So please stop acting like it."

I placed the cup back on my desk and rose. "Maybe we should go to the police."

Jacques gave me a gentle pushed back into the chair. "Are you nuts? Call your friend Aaron instead. See if he can find out anything. If you start asking questions or let on that you knew her, you could wind up a suspect. Does that sound familiar?"

He was right. When a former coworker had been murdered a few months ago and I'd stumbled upon her dead body, all fingers had pointed in my direction. Living in such a small town, this new incident would not exactly make me look like an innocent bystander.

"What did Mildred say in her phone message to you?"

I forced myself to take a sip of tea. "She said that she remembered something. It had to be the name on the piece of paper in Paul's hand. Maybe it links to the conversation Paul had with her."

Jacques pursed his lips. "Stop and think about this for a minute. Maybe you were wrong. Maybe Paul did commit suicide. Perhaps he found out he was sick or couldn't father kids. Would that have left him devastated enough to kill himself?"

I forced back a laugh. "Jacques, that's ridiculous! And if he had committed suicide, why would someone have reason to kill Mildred?"

He scratched his head thoughtfully. "Well, that's true enough. And it certainly proves we're on the right track. So someone killed him, discovered Mildred had information, and they killed her too." Jacques snapped his fingers. "Maybe he asked Mildred about the infertility because he wanted to be a donor. They get paid well. No, wait, that can't be right. He didn't need the money."

I leaned forward eagerly. "I wouldn't go that far. Paul confided to me that his parents expected him to contribute to his living expenses at college. And he worried about having time for a job in addition to his studies. Maybe he did ask her how he could go about the process."

Jacques folded his arms across his chest. "I suppose that works. Now let's get back to what else Rachel said. Do you think she was telling the truth about Paul and Michelle being involved?"

The thought of Paul being with Michelle was enough to start the nausea moving in my stomach again. "Like I said before, I can't see it. Paul wouldn't have done that to his brother, even if Ben and Michelle were broken up at the time. Maybe I need to place a call to Carl Williams."

"The quarterback?"

I nodded. "The twins were invited to a birthday party for his daughter a few months back. They were in the same class last year. I think I still have his number on my phone."

Jacques nodded in approval. "I'll leave you alone then. Make sure you fax the contract over to Marcia Steele right away. We need attorney approval as soon as possible. I'll be in my office catching up on some cold-calling if you need me."

Cold-calling was a process pretty much the same as telemarketing. Real estate agents would call people whose listings had recently expired or those that were represented by the owner themselves—for sale by owners, or FSBO—and convince the customers to give them a try. As a result of the process, I received dozens of hang-ups in my ear every month. Jacques, though, was an expert at cold-calling. He had that type of voice that people trusted and would stop and listen to.

I reached for my phone. "I was going to give Marcia a quick

call first and let her know it was on the way. Then I'll send it over."

Marcia Steele was a real estate attorney who I recommended to all of my clients. I'd worked with her before on several occasions. She was honest, fair, and one of the best in the business at doing title searches. I'd been surprised when Ben and Michelle had asked for an attorney recommendation the other day. Since he was a lawyer himself, I assumed Ben might have someone he preferred to use, but he had eagerly accepted my suggestion of Marcia. Perhaps Ben didn't have many friends left in the business after the rumors with his young intern surfaced.

I opened the folder that contained the contract, just in case Marcia had any questions, and scrolled under the contacts in my phone for her number. Fortunately, she was in the office that morning. We chatted briefly, but when I mentioned Ben's name, she grew silent for a few seconds. Finally, she found her voice again.

"Really," she snorted on the other end of the line. "I don't like to talk bad about fellow attorneys, but I've heard the rumors about this guy and his promiscuity. I wouldn't doubt for a moment that's the reason for his early retirement. I mean, think about it, Cindy. You and I are in our early forties, and God knows I'm in no condition to retire yet. I figure it'll be at least another ten years for me. How about you?"

"Um, a little longer," I replied. Yeah, probably closer to thirty years for me. "Are you sure you're okay with representing them at the closing? If it makes you uncomfortable, I can find someone else. No hard feelings."

"Oh it's fine," Marcia said dryly. "A sale is a sale, and this should be an easy one. Let's face it, kiddo, a few of the ones you've sent me in the past have made me want to rip my hair out. So this one pales in comparison."

We laughed together and talked for a few more minutes,

then made plans to get together for lunch next week before I disconnected. Afterward, I went downstairs to use the scanner and then came back to my office to email the contract to Marcia. I scrolled through the contact section of my phone again. There was a number for Carl Williams that I assumed was his home phone. I doubted I'd catch him there since it was a work day, but I could always leave a message.

"Carl Williams. How can I help you?"

His response caught me by surprise, and I had to think for a moment. "Hi Carl, it's Cindy York. I hope I'm not catching you at a bad time."

Carl laughed. "Nah, it's fine. Just another boring day at work. How's the real estate gig going? I heard that the market isn't doing well."

"It's improving," I mumbled, not knowing what else to say.

"Say, Natalie wants to have a pool party next week and invite the twins. Probably on Saturday. Hope they can make it."

"They'll be thrilled, I'm sure." I hesitated, still not quite sure how to broach the subject. "Um, I didn't see you at the reunion the other night."

He paused. "Ah, no. I err—couldn't make it. Did you have a good time at the stuffy, pretentious Steadman mansion?"

Oh boy. I sensed the green-eyed monster looming. I also knew that Carl and his wife had filed for bankruptcy recently. I decided to cut right to the chase. "Why couldn't you make it? Were you afraid to see Michelle again?"

Carl's voice turned sharp. "Cindy, where are you going with this?"

Having no choice, I continued. "I found out some information the other night at the reunion that leads me to believe Paul Steadman did not commit suicide. I'm convinced he was murdered."

The silence on the other end was long and deafening. "What

are you trying to say? Do you think I had something to do with his murder?"

"That's not what I was implying."

"Look, I was angry when Paul found us together, but I never would have killed the guy."

My ears pricked up with this sudden revelation. "Paul found you and Michelle together? In a compromising position?"

Carl sighed. "I figured he'd told you since you guys were so close. Ben had broken up with her, and she was in a tough state. She asked me if I'd go to Nick Keller's party with her. Almost the entire class was there—including your buddy, Paul. I don't remember seeing you though."

I paused and tried to collect my thoughts. Nick was always throwing parties when his parents went out of town, which was quite often. "If that was in late May, I had the flu."

"Okay, I'll be honest. Michelle was really vulnerable that night, so I didn't hesitate to take advantage of her. One thing led to another, and we went upstairs to…ah…get comfortable in one of the bedrooms. You remember how teenage guys could be." He chuckled.

Ew. This is why I'd always hated those kind of parties.

He went on before I could muster a reply. "In my defense, I was crazy about her. We dated before she and Ben hooked up."

"I know."

"Anyhow, I think Paul was looking for the bathroom, but he walked into the wrong room and found us—um—involved. And boy, was he pissed. Yelled that she was a money-grubbing slut. I mean, what gave him the right to judge? He and his brother didn't even like each other. Plus, Ben and Michelle were broken up at the time. Michelle was really upset about it."

I bristled inwardly. "Paul was very protective of his family. And maybe he didn't know that they were broken up. From what I understand, the separation was brief. And in the meantime, Michelle jumps right into bed with you?"

Carl breathed heavily on the other end. "My. Sounds like you're judgmental too."

A tingle of uneasiness ran through me. "I'm not trying to be. I know you cared about her. But it seems like this all happened pretty fast."

He made a harrumphing sound. "Look, I don't have to explain anything to you. Hell, if she was free now I might even seek her out again. But she's got everything she wants, so why would she ever give me the time of day? No offense, but I was having a pretty good morning until you called. Is there anything else?"

Nice going, Cin. You've succeeded in royally pissing this guy off. I was about to say good-bye when another thought struck me. Hey, why not go for broke? "You were planning to become a doctor, weren't you?"

"That was my initial goal, yes. But my grades weren't good enough. Some of us weren't born to be straight-A students, no matter how hard we worked. So now I'm stuck at a 9-to-5 job where I can barely make ends meet."

I was afraid to ask my next question. "Didn't you ask Paul to recommend you for a job at the hospital?"

Carl snorted. "Yeah, I wanted to be a certified nursing assistant. I thought that might be a good way to get my foot in the door on the way to becoming an MD eventually. And Paul knew many of the senior doctors there. So as soon as he got in, I asked for a favor."

"But he refused to recommend you."

Another long, uncomfortable silence followed. "Hey, I just remembered. The party's cancelled for next week." With that, Carl disconnected.

I leaned back in my chair, pondering this new information. It had never dawned on me before that Paul might have enemies. He was an incredibly sweet and down-to-earth guy. True, he could be pushy at times and was never shy about asking questions. That's how I was convinced he would have made a great doctor. Plus, he was loyal to his friends and family. Jealousy could be a deadly thing though. Yes, Carl had disliked Paul and was obviously envious of him. He also hated Ben for stealing away the girl that he had loved. But was that enough of a motive to want Paul dead?

My phone buzzed, jerking me out of my thoughts. The number on the screen was unfamiliar. "This is Cindy. How may I assist you?"

"Cindy, it's Doctor Sanchez. Do you have a few minutes?"

"Oh, Doctor! I was going to call you later. What's up?"

He hesitated. "Uh, I have the result of your tests from yesterday."

The doctor sounded a bit off, and suddenly, I found myself worrying if something might be wrong with me. "Are they— I mean— Is everything okay?"

Doctor Sanchez paused for a few seconds, just long enough for me to realize that no, everything was not okay. "You don't have an ulcer."

"Oh." I found myself oddly disappointed. "So, I'm guessing that my other theory was correct. It *is* the change."

"No, Cindy, it's not the change."

His voice sounded ominous, and the hairs on the back of my neck stood at attention. There *was* something wrong with me. *Oh my God.* Everyone had been talking about cancer lately. Was that it? I convinced myself that it couldn't be breast cancer because I hadn't had a recent mammogram. They had taken blood, though. So what had shown up on the test?

"Cindy, are you still there?"

Like a sharp-beaked bird, fear began to peck away at me. I braced myself for the news. "Doctor Sanchez, how long do I have?"

Much to my surprise, he laughed out loud. "Cindy, you're not dying. In fact, you're in excellent health. I was wondering if you might want to come into the office this afternoon so I could tell you the news in person. Maybe around two o'clock or so."

Okay, so if I wasn't dying, what else was there? I found my impatience growing. "Doctor Sanchez, just tell me what's going on. Please."

"You're pregnant."

CHAPTER SIXTEEN

I shook my head at the phone and laughed. "Okay, Doctor. Nice try. It's not April Fool's, so let's hear the real diagnosis, please."

A shocked silence met me. "Cindy, I would never joke around with a patient like that. From what I can tell, you're about seven weeks along."

Panic engulfed me as his words set in, and I found myself struggling to breathe normally. "No. You've *got* to be wrong, Doctor. That's impossible."

"I know this comes as a shock, but I can assure you that you're definitely pregnant."

I glanced down at the floor. There was an enormous black hole waiting to swallow me up, and for a moment, I was tempted to let it. "But I can't be. I'm too old."

He clucked his tongue against the roof of his mouth, which only irritated me further. "You're not too old. I have another patient who's going to be fifty in a few months. Some women put off pregnancy until later in life so that they can have a career first."

But I'm over forty, have three kids already, and *no* real career to speak of. Tears slid down my cheeks onto my desk, creating a small puddle. "Oh my God. I can't do this, Doctor. I just can't."

He was quiet on the other end of the line, and I was immediately ashamed of my outburst. A baby was a gift. Some women would give their right arm for a child, and here I was, acting like a spoiled brat who couldn't have her own way.

"Talk to Greg. I'm sure he'll be thrilled."

Greg! I stifled another sob. No, I was pretty certain that Greg would *not* be thrilled. Hadn't Greg mentioned how happy he was that the kids were getting older so we could have a little time to ourselves now? "I don't know how this could have happened."

"The usual way, Cindy."

I could feel Doctor Sanchez smiling on the other end while my face heated. "No, I mean—I always use protection. I never forget to take it. This has to be some type of mistake."

"Nothing is foolproof besides abstinence. You know that. Now, I have a patient waiting, but if you'd like to come in for a chat, let me know. How about I schedule you for an appointment to come in and speak with someone about your options. And I'm calling in a prescription for prenatal vitamins too. I'd like to see you back in the office in two to three weeks for an exam. We can talk more then."

"But— Doctor, I can't—"

His voice was gentle. "You're going to be fine, Cindy. I'll speak with you soon." He clicked off without another word.

I placed the phone down on my desk. I was dimly aware of the wall clock ticking away the precious minutes, hours of my life. How did that old soap opera theme go? *Like sand through the hourglass, these are the days of our lives.*

I wasn't sure how long I sat there, staring into space. Time no longer held any relevance for me as the doctor's words had already sealed my fate.

I'm going to have another baby.

Seven weeks along. I racked my brain. Oh God. Our anniversary. I remembered drinking too much at dinner, coming home to drink some more, Greg's mention of my strip-tease that night, and I vaguely recalled what we had done afterward. It had been a perfect evening. Had I remembered to take my pill that morning? I shut my eyes and tried to recall the details from earlier that day.

The kids had just finished the school year. I had gone into the kitchen that morning and heard the twins screaming from downstairs. There was a mouse in the house, and Rusty and Sweetie had both been chasing it. Rusty had crashed into a table and broken some glasses that were standing on it. After I had cleaned up the mess, Jacques called about a client who needed to see a house that morning. I had flown up the stairs to get dressed in a hurry. When I came home later that afternoon, I'd fixed an early dinner for the kids, and then we'd dropped them off at Helen's house for the night.

My heart sank to the pit of my stomach. Yes, I could have forgotten.

When I found out I was expecting Darcy, it was a joy. We'd both been so excited. The twins had been a surprise but nevertheless more blessings as well. And now this. I would be sixty-two when this child graduated from high school. Time to think about retirement, not college tuition and teaching kids how to drive.

Darcy would be turning sixteen next month and was already talking about the type of vehicle she wanted. She'd be lucky if we could afford any type of lemon at this rate, with the rust costing extra. We barely made ends meet as it was, so how could we possibly afford another baby on top of everything else?

"Are you listening to me?"

I looked up to see Jacques standing in the doorway. "Huh?"

He waved a shaft of papers at me. "New listing. Not as prestigious as Ben and Michelle's but close. I told you their house was going to be our saving grace. It also didn't hurt when I told my new client that it pended sale only after three days too."

I turned away and gave my eyes a subtle swipe with the back of my hand. "That's great."

He frowned and came around the desk to stare down at me. "You need to stop blaming yourself about Mildred. It's not your—"

I placed my face in my hands and started to sob. "I'm pregnant."

Jacques gasped out loud, and then there was silence in the room for a few beats. I glanced up, curious for his reaction, and saw him watching me, his expression grim.

"You know," he said. "I did kind of wonder about that."

I stared back at him in confusion. "How could you think I might be pregnant when it never even crossed *my* mind? Are you psychic now?"

His mouth twitched at the corners. "I'm very perceptive that way."

I wiped my eyes again. "What the heck am I going to do? Greg won't be happy."

He handed me a handkerchief. "Look, darling, I realize this is a shock and all, but your man loves you, and that won't change, baby or no baby."

I straightened up and blew my nose. "I know that. But there are other things to consider beside Greg not being happy. We can barely afford to feed the three we have now. And I'm over forty, Jacques. We'll be ready for Geritol when it's time to send this kid to college. And what if there's something wrong with the baby because of my age? I'm scared."

Jacques hesitated for a moment. "I hate to bring this up, but if you're really that miserable about your—ah—predicament, there are other options, you know."

I shook my head furiously. "Not for me. I can't do that."

He tapped a pen against his teeth. "Don't they say that once you have one set of twins, the likelihood for another set triples or something?"

"Oh my God." I started sobbing again.

He leaned down and placed his arms around me. "Cin, you should be happy! You know that you can always bring the baby to work with you. I'll support you in any way that I can. Darcy's old enough to help too. And I'll babysit. It will be good for Ed. Maybe even convince him that we need a child in our lives too."

"I thought you two were getting ready to adopt?"

The smile on his face faded. "Ed keeps putting it off. I know his career is important to him, but family comes first with me. That's where we differ."

I reached up to grab his hand. "Is everything okay between the two of you?"

He squeezed mine in return. "Oh, sure. Ed and I will be just fine."

There was something implied in his tone that made me wonder if he was telling the truth, but I didn't press the issue. Jacques was private about his personal life, even with me.

He lifted me out of the chair and wrapped me in a bear hug. "And you're going to be fine too."

I clung to my dear friend, sobbing into his shoulder. I was ashamed of my feelings. There were so many women in this world who longed for a child and could never have one. But I felt drained and worn out. After the twins, we'd decided we were done having kids. This little unplanned surprise had never been on my radar screen. And as much as Greg loved me and our children, I sensed this was not in his plans either.

Someone coughed in the doorway. "Excuse me." Our receptionist, Linda Earl, was standing there, looking uncomfortable as she watched our embrace. She was a very attractive woman in her mid-twenties.

Jacques released me. "Yes, Linda, what is it?"

"There's a gentleman downstairs asking questions about one

of your listings. Would you like me to put him in your office or the conference room?"

He stared at me, but I shook my head and gestured toward the door. "Go. We'll talk later. I'll be fine, don't worry."

He gave me a sharp look and then winked. "I'll be back in a few minutes, dear, and then I'm going to take you to lunch."

I blew my nose again with Jacques' handkerchief and sat back down in my chair. I appreciated his words and thanked my lucky stars for such a wonderful friend. But the truth of the matter was that I was still shell-shocked.

My cell phone buzzed. I stared down at the screen, and both my stomach and heart lurched with dread. My husband.

I lifted the phone in my trembling hands. What was I going to say to him? *Sorry, honey, but your overactive libido caught up with us. How do you feel about 2:00 am feedings again?*

If I didn't answer the phone, I was only prolonging the inevitable. Plus, he was worried about my health, so if I didn't pick up, he'd think something was wrong. I blew out a long, steady breath. "Hello?"

"Hey." His voice was warm and sexy on the other end. "How's my favorite girl this morning?"

I swallowed hard, trying to force the tears back down in my throat. "Fine."

There was a silence. "What's wrong?"

Gee, where should I start? *The woman I went to see the other day was strangled to death this morning, and I'm pretty sure it's my fault.* Or maybe I should just cut right to the chase. *Guess who's going to be a daddy again?*

"Nothing," I lied. "I'm just tired." I was a true wimp in the sense of the word but thought it might be better to wait and do this face to face so I could gauge his reaction. "Do you think we could go out to dinner tonight?"

Greg sighed. "I wish. That's why I'm calling. Bill Freedman was supposed to attend the trade show in Syracuse tonight, but he's ill. He asked me if I'd go in his place. I'm packing a bag and then heading out. Darcy will take care of the boys, so there's no need for you to rush home. Are you at the office or off monitoring those inspections?"

The butterflies in my stomach moved at full force, and made me nauseous. At least now I knew why I was queasy all the time. "No, those are tomorrow morning. So... You're going away again?"

"It's just for one evening, baby. I'll be back tomorrow night. And Bill's going to take the show for me in August. So I won't be going anywhere for a while, promise."

Tears filled my eyes again. "I don't want you to go."

He purred into the phone. "You know what I've been thinking? You and I need some alone time. A vacation, for just the two of us. Now that you've sold the Steadman mansion, I think we should put some cash away from that deal, and then you and I will jet off for a long weekend to Florida or maybe even the Bahamas this coming winter. How does that sound?"

Let's see. Next winter, I'd be about seven months pregnant. I hoped we could afford an extra plane ticket because I'd be taking up two seats by then. "Um—well, it's definitely something to think about."

Greg was quiet on the other end. "Sweetheart, there's something you're not telling me. Are you sick again? Did the doctor call?"

I couldn't give him the news now. I was afraid he might steer his car off the Thruway in a moment of sheer panic. "Yes, he called. And I'm not sick." At least I wasn't lying.

"Well, that's great. I was starting to worry. So, does he think it's...you know, menopause?"

"It's definitely not the change." *And how.*

"That's wonderful. Listen, I have to run. I'll call you tonight, okay?"

"Greg?"

"What?"

I fought the sudden urge to weep again. "I love you."

"Love you too, baby. Talk to you tonight."

With that, he was gone.

I set the phone down on my desk and turned to stare out the window at the brilliant sunlight shimmering through the glass. It was only noon, and already the day had shaped up to be a strange one. I wouldn't be able to tell Greg until I saw him tomorrow night, so it was pointless to be concerned about that right now. There would be plenty of time to worry later. Hopefully, the inspections would go off without a hitch, and in a few weeks, I'd have my commission check. We really needed the money now.

My thoughts returned to Mildred, and I shivered, reaching for my sweater on the back of my chair, despite the warm summer day outside. I was convinced my theory about Paul was correct. And I was wracked with guilt that this sweet woman had died because she had wanted to share information with me.

I ran over the list of suspects in my head again. Rachel was my top pick. But how would she have known I was going to see Mildred? Melanie fit into the category as well. She'd once had a one-night stand with Ben years ago and still had an axe to grind. Plus, she knew about Mildred. Carl Williams? It was possible, but I just didn't see it. And sadly, I couldn't rule out Ben, as much as I wanted to.

Was there something or someone else I was overlooking? And why had Paul been interested in sterility and talking to Mildred about it? Whose name was on that piece of paper in Paul's hand? Was it a note of some sort?

Jacques appeared in the doorway, dangling his car keys. "Ready to go, love?"

I eased myself out of the chair. "I'm really not that hungry."

He waggled an admonishing finger at me. "Don't give me

that. You need to keep up your strength. You're eating for two now. Maybe even three."

I groaned. "Fine. But afterward, drop me off at my house. I have to set up showings for a client for next week, and I might as well do it from there. Plus, I feel like I've been neglecting the kids lately."

He slung an arm around my shoulders as we walked outside to his vehicle. "That's the beauty of this job, dear. You can make your own hours and work from home whenever you like. It's perfect for someone in your condition."

Ugh. I winced. "Jacques, I really hate that term. It makes me sound like I have a disease or something. I'm having a baby, not dying."

It felt weird saying the words out loud, and I glanced at my friend with apprehension. "It would be great if I could bring the baby with me to work."

"I told you, that's fine. You can have anything you want, darling, as long as you are present and accountable for at the house inspections tomorrow morning. Oh, and I just received a call about that condo I listed last week. Some Donald Trump-wannabe from out of town is dying to look at it, and nine o'clock tomorrow morning is the only time he's available. So I need you to be at the Steadmans'—alert, smiling, and hopefully not puking your guts out."

"You say the most eloquent things. I won't let you down, I promise."

"Good. He nodded in approval as he opened the passenger side door for me. "And one more thing."

"Yes?"

"If it's a boy, you'll name it after me, right?"

I had to laugh. "Don't push your luck."

CHAPTER SEVENTEEN

"Okay, guys, upstairs to take your showers." I lifted the dinner dishes off the table and stacked them in the sink. "Darcy, would you—"

She gave a small toss of her head. "I know. Do the dishes. Cripes, some days I feel like I'm Cinderella around here."

"You're not dirty enough," Seth pointed out. "Come on out back with us, and we'll show you how to make mud pies."

"Yeah, we'll throw one right in your face," Stevie added.

I reached for my cup of herbal tea and sat back down in my chair. "Knock it off, guys. Upstairs, now." I pointed in the direction of the living room.

They grumbled as they lifted the puppy in the air and walked out of the room. A few seconds later I heard them thumping up the staircase and the dog barking. "And please do not bring Rusty into the shower with you again!"

I glanced up to see my daughter's huge, dark eyes fixated on mine.

"What is it?" I asked.

She frowned. "You really look terrible. I don't think you're getting enough exercise."

I almost started to laugh, except the topic wasn't quite funny. "You could be right. Maybe I'll take up roller skating." My intent was to be humorous, but my daughter didn't seem amused.

Darcy placed a dish in the drainer. "Michelle is a vegetarian. She has fish and salad every night. Maybe that should be your diet."

I sighed and said nothing, clutching the cup between my hands. A few more days and Michelle and Ben would be out of our lives for good. How I was starting to look forward to that.

"By the way, don't forget. Michelle is coming to pick me up tomorrow when her inspections are done. Unless I can ride over to the house with you."

I shook my head. "Darcy, I'm sorry, but with everything else going on today, I guess I forgot to tell you. I need you to watch your brothers tomorrow."

She whirled her head around, surprised. "What about Grandma?"

"I told you, I don't like asking your grandmother all of the time."

Angrily, she threw a dish in the drainer, and I winced, afraid she might have broken it. "You're a liar. You just don't want me around Michelle because you're jealous of her."

I reached deep down inside for some patience, but after everything that had happened earlier today, my tank was running on empty. "It's not what you think." I didn't want to tell her the real truth, which is that I was afraid Ben might have something to do with Paul's death. And what if Michelle knew about it all these years and was protecting her husband? Nausea washed over me again. The further my daughter stayed away from them, the better.

"Oh, bullshit. You're jealous. She told me in high school you were always jealous of her."

A bolt of anger shot through me, and I got to my feet. "You

know better than to use such language in this house. And what exactly did Michelle tell you?"

Darcy bore a triumphant smile. "She said that you were like all the rest of the girls back then. You knew you couldn't have Ben, so you settled for his brother."

I sucked in a sharp breath. "Paul and I were friends. That's all."

My daughter laughed. "Michelle told me you'd say that. And she also said that the real truth was that Paul was always going around trying to make trouble for everyone. He was too nosy for his own good. Then she said that maybe he got what was coming to him. Sounds like it to me."

The room spun out of focus for a moment. I couldn't believe the hateful words coming out of my daughter's mouth. When had she become so filled with venom? I raised my hand in the air but stopped myself just in time. I'd never struck her before and wasn't about to start now.

I narrowed my eyes at her. Darcy took a step back and I watched as an expression of fear moved over her face.

My voice shook slightly. "I can't believe you would say such hateful things about a man you never even knew. I'll finish the dishes. Go to your room because, as of this moment, you're grounded. And I will personally tell Michelle tomorrow morning that she won't be seeing you again."

She flung the dish cloth across the room and burst into tears. "That's so typical of you. You always have to ruin everything. I wish Daddy was here."

I folded my arms across my chest. "No, you don't, because he would agree with me."

"I hate you so much." She flew out of the room, and stomped angrily up the stairs. Within a minute I heard the door to her bedroom slam.

Sighing, I went to the sink and finished the dishes, my hands trembling. Client or no client, Michelle was going to hear a few things from me tomorrow. I was glad for a chance to keep myself busy because on the inside, rage was boiling over at a furious pace.

After I finished stacking the dishes, I heard a scratch at the back door and went to let Sweetie in. Her food dish was empty, so I filled it and gave her fresh water while she purred and rubbed against my legs. At least there was one female in this house who still liked me.

I stared down at my phone screen and noticed I'd missed a call from Greg. Damn. I'd placed it on mute earlier and forgotten to change it back again. Quickly, I dialed my voice-mail, anxious to hear his voice.

"Hey, baby. I'm off to dinner with a couple of prospective clients. Looks like I may get a good-sized account out of this. Fingers crossed. I'll try calling you back if it's not too late when I get in, but they're talking about drinks afterward. Oh." He chuckled low into the phone. "Look under your pillow. I left you a little present for our upcoming trip this winter. Can't wait to see you in it. Love you."

I was sorry to have missed his call. I could have used his sound advice about Darcy right now. Most of the time, Greg handled her better than I did. I felt so alone at the moment. Even though I dreaded telling him the news about the baby, I wanted him with me.

I climbed the stairs again and glanced into the twins' room. Seth was lying on his bed with Rusty, and Stevie was in the bathroom taking his shower. Loud rock music was blaring from Darcy's room, another sign that she was furious with me. Not in the mood to confront her again, I chose to ignore the noise and went into my room, closing the door firmly behind me.

There was a small, flat package under the pillow that I guessed was lingerie. I lifted the top and removed the tissue paper.

Oh no.

In the box was a two piece, bright aqua-colored bikini and a note from Greg. *Oh, the fun I'm going to have when you wear this. Maybe another striptease? Love you.*

Good grief. I put the top back on the box. Sure, I'd wear it next winter when we were alone in a tropical paradise. Poor Greg might have nightmares afterward though. I laughed, in spite of myself, then opened the top drawer of my nightstand and placed the box inside. I left the note on top and shut the drawer. Secretly, I hoped that Helen would look in there again the next time she babysat. I pictured her reaction and, my sour mood instantly improved.

As I descended the stairs, I caught the musical notes of my cell and rushed into the kitchen, hoping it was Greg. No such luck. I pressed the button. "Hello, this is Cindy."

"Cindy, Aaron Connors here. Sorry I wasn't available when you called earlier. You sounded upset. What's going on?"

I went into the study and shut the door behind me, not wanting the kids to overhear. I quickly explained to Aaron about Mildred and what had transpired. He whistled low in his throat.

"Have you heard anything about her death?" I asked.

"No, but I can find out easily enough. Look, as far as I'm concerned, this proves your theory about Paul was correct. I'm just sorry this woman had to suffer as a result. Not to change the subject, but I was going to call you anyway. I have the DNA results on Paul's hat back."

With everything else that had happened lately, I'd forgotten all about the hat. I crossed my fingers. "That was quick. Did they find anything?"

"No matches in the DNA bank. All that means is that the person didn't have a criminal record. There were some hair samples though. Paul was dark haired, correct?"

"That's right."

He coughed. "We found a blonde hair, so it's possible the

sample might have belonged to his killer. Did anyone in his family have light hair?"

"No. They were all dark." I tried to fight off the despair threatening to overwhelm me. This was the only piece of evidence, and we'd just hit a major snag. "So, there's no way to figure out who did this?"

"Unless you have some suspects already. Any ideas?"

"Well, I did go and visit Rachel Kennedy. I thought she might have been the one who did this, except you told me she'd been arrested in the past, so—"

Aaron interrupted. "Then there would have been a match." He clicked his tongue against the roof of his mouth for what seemed like an eternity. "Unless the hair didn't belong to the killer."

The answer seemed to be right there for my taking, but I couldn't quite put my finger on it. "Can you find out any more details about how Mildred died? Like I said, we're pretty sure it was strangulation, but maybe you could check if the police have any leads or found any additional evidence?"

The tongue clicking resumed, so I knew Aaron was mulling this over. "I'm having lunch with a former colleague of mine tomorrow, so I'll run it by him. Cindy, you're not going to like this suggestion, but you should really go down to the station and tell the police what you know."

"What if they think it was me? I'd just been to see Mildred the day before."

"I'll back your claim up. You don't need to worry about that. But it's time to get the police involved. They may decide to reopen the investigation."

"After all this time?"

"It's a possibility. Nothing is ever a done deal. I think they're going to want to hear everything that you know, starting with the note Paul wrote you."

I sighed. I knew he was right, but that didn't make me feel

any better. "All right. I'm tied up tomorrow morning, but I'll go over in the afternoon."

"I'm glad to hear it. And I'll be in touch as soon as I know anything about Miss Reynolds' death."

As I placed the phone in my pocket, there was a scratching coming from the other side of the door. I opened it to find the twins standing there with Rusty between them.

"What were you doing on the phone? Were you talking to Daddy?" Stevie asked.

"How come I never get to talk to him?" Seth demanded. "You're always hogging Dad on the phone."

"What do you guys talk about? How to make more babies?" Stevie asked.

Oh no. This again. "Did you guys brush your teeth?"

"Yes," they both said in unison.

"Okay, upstairs to bed. I'll be there to read to you in a minute. Go pick out something from your bookcase. And no Harry Potter."

"Can't we read from *The Prisoner of Azkaban?*" Seth pleaded.

I shook my head. "That stuff will give you nightmares."

"Not me," Stevie said. "I always sleep great after I read about Harry. I wish I was him. That'd be awesome."

"Okay then, it gives *me* nightmares. Now, go find something else, like Doctor Seuss."

"That's for babies!" Stevie protested. He pointed at Rusty, who was now at the kitchen door, whining. "Rusty has to pee."

I sighed. "Okay. I'll take care of Rusty. Is your sister still in her room?"

Stevie nodded. "She's playing Justin Bieber now. That must mean she's mad at you again."

No doubt. If there was one thing I disliked more than heavy metal, it was Justin Bieber, and my daughter knew this. Darcy was great at getting under my skin these days. "Tell her to turn the music down because you're going to bed." I gave them each a slight swat on the behind. "Get moving."

They raced each other up the staircase while Rusty continued to whine. I grabbed his leash off the kitchen wall. "Okay, come on, boy."

We exited through the kitchen door, which led us to the back of the house. There was a small fenced yard with an area designated for Rusty—dog pen, house, and water bowl. He never spent much time out here except for when he had to do his doggie business. Rusty whined loudly whenever he was away from the twins, and we didn't want the neighbors to hate us.

I was grateful that Greg had cleaned out his pen earlier. I left Rusty in the fenced area and walked back around to the front of the house, enjoying a brief moment to examine the full moon that illuminated the darkened sky. It was a beautiful summer night. The air was warm but without the recent humidity. Crickets chirped nearby, and I smelled honeysuckle. I leaned against the garage and closed my eyes for a second.

One week ago, my life had been simple or at least compared to what I was dealing with now. I hadn't known the truth about Paul, although, looking back, I should have realized he never would have committed suicide. A woman was dead as a result of my snooping. A week ago, I hadn't known I was pregnant. My daughter and I had been getting along well. Now, like a train wreck, my life had suddenly veered off track, and I wondered if it would ever right itself again.

I placed my hands over my stomach. I wanted to feel happy and excited about this baby yet couldn't bring myself to do it. Maybe the doctor was right, and I should speak with someone. But the first thing I had to do was share the bombshell with my husband. I prayed that Greg would take the news better than me but had my doubts.

As I started toward the backyard to grab Rusty, my gaze

shifted to the car. I had backed it into the driveway the night before. With the moon cascading over the front of the vehicle, I noticed something seemed off. I walked down the driveway for a closer look and then sucked in a sharp breath.

The car's front windshield was shattered. At first, I wondered if it might have been from the heat. I hadn't driven the vehicle today and had forgotten to leave the windows open a crack, something Greg always admonished me about in hot weather. But the oppressive heat had subsided earlier in the week, so I didn't think that was the cause.

With trepidation, I approached the car, as if fearful it might burst into flames at any second. A piece of paper had been affixed under the windshield wiper. Blood pounded through my veins as I removed the slip and read the message that had obviously been left for my eyes.

Déjà Vu, bitch.

CHAPTER EIGHTEEN

*I*t was ten minutes past nine the next morning when I pulled into the driveway of the sprawling Steadman estate. As usual, I was late and winced when I spotted Michelle's corvette, Tricia's Audi, and the buyer's BMW already there, along with the inspector's van. Jacques would have a cow if he found out I'd been the last one to arrive.

I'd been forced to call my mother-in-law that morning and grovel, pleading with her to come over and then on top of everything else, asking to borrow her car. Helen had been surprisingly cooperative for once, something that puzzled me. She'd also looked at me with a sly smile, almost as if she was aware something was going on. Was she privy to my little secret? Women's intuition, by chance? *Great.* That would be all I needed, especially if she got to Greg before I did.

First thing that morning, I'd called the insurance company. Fortunately, we had glass coverage, and a local company would be coming out shortly to repair my windshield. I decided to wait and report the incident to the police that afternoon when I went down to the station. I didn't want them coming to the house so that Helen could witness our exchange. I'd laughed the incident off to my mother-in-law, explaining some kids were probably just fooling around.

Deep down inside, I knew that was a lie.

I was convinced this was the same person who'd shattered my windshield years ago. And that person had been Rachel. At the time, a friend had mentioned they'd seen her car on my street that night, but no one had witnessed her in the act. However, Rachel's statement the other night convinced me she had been the one to commit the deed.

Sure, Rachel had been obsessed with Paul, but could she actually be his killer? The hair the lab found hadn't been a match with hers. And there were plenty of people who'd known about my windshield back then as I'd been forced to drive it like that until I could get it fixed. Gossip had always spread like wildfire in my town—and high school.

My head was spinning. I hadn't slept well last night and had brought Rusty into my room for company. I should have called the police but didn't want the kids to wake up and wonder what horrible thing had happened. I decided I'd go down to the station this afternoon and tell the police everything then.

As I'd lain in bed, idly listening to old reruns on the television for hours, I thought that the person who had done this to my vehicle must be the one responsible for Paul's death. What if this lunatic tried to harm my children next?

I had phoned Jacques before I left the house that morning, but the call went immediately to voicemail. I hadn't left a message. The last thing Jacques wanted to hear right now was that I didn't have transportation to the Steadmans'. He needed to know he could depend on me. And after everything Jacques had done for me in the past, I wasn't about to let him down. Being left with no other alternative, I'd phoned my mother-in-law.

Right now, all I wanted was to get the inspections over with and head home to my children.

I grabbed my briefcase and hurried toward the front door. As I stepped into the entranceway, I stared in shock at the surroundings.

The Steadmans had wasted no time. From what I could see, all of the furniture had been removed. There were a couple of chairs left in the drawing room, probably as a courtesy for the buyers. A coffee pot and mugs had been set out on a small folding table next to it.

Tricia was standing next to the staircase, talking to her buyers. As if on cue, they all turned and looked at me, and I noticed the smiles vanish from their faces in a hurry.

With trepidation, I glanced down at my skirt. What was wrong this time? I had dressed in a hurry that morning. No, everything seemed to be in place clothing wise. Oh, cripes. They were looking at my face. Along with everything else, I'd been sick again that morning. Maybe Helen had heard me retching, and that's why she'd been nice to me afterward. Or perhaps because she hoped I was dying.

"Hi there," I greeted them. "Sorry I'm late."

Tricia gave a toss of her stringy, dishwater blonde hair. I knew that gesture well. It was her disparaging way of indicating that my presence didn't matter.

"I thought Jacques would be here," she said snidely. "But then again, he's always on time."

Ah yes, she was anything but subtle.

The two owners of Safety First Inspections walked out from the kitchen, and I greeted them, happy for a distraction. I'd worked with brothers Fred and Bob Gilson several times before. They were perhaps the most reputable team of home inspectors in our area.

"We're going outside to check the condition of the roof, if you'd like to tag along," Fred said to the buyers.

The Whitakers looked at Tricia, who gestured for them to go

ahead. "I'll be right along. I need to speak with Cindy for a moment."

Great. Here it comes.

She waited until the four of them had disappeared and then glared at me. "I guess a seven-figure sale means nothing to you because you have so many of them, right?"

I folded my arms across my chest. I was in no mood for a lecture from her right now. "Tricia, I was ten minutes late. I had car trouble, plus I was sick this morning. So sue me."

She snickered and took a step back. "Well, I hope it's not contagious, because you look like a pile of dog poo." She paused as Michelle started down the staircase toward us. "Now there's a woman with class and beauty. One we should all aspire to be like."

"Ah, you're such a phony," I muttered. "Go babysit your clients. I need to talk to Michelle. *Alone.*"

Her mouth fell open as she regarded me in amazement. I'd rendered her speechless, something that didn't happen often. I never spoke to other agents that way, but I was tired of Tricia's high-and-mighty attitude. Michelle caught the tail end of our conversation and also stared at me in surprise.

"Well, really," Tricia huffed. "I can't wait to tell Jacques about your unprofessional attitude. You're a disgrace to the business."

I shrugged. "Feel free. But you need to go outside. *Now.*"

Both of them observed me in silence for a moment, and then Tricia turned on her heel. "You haven't heard the last from me, Mrs. York."

"Does anyone?" I called after her.

I turned my attention to Michelle. She was dressed casually in white shorts and a pink lace tank top, her blonde hair in a single braid down her back, making her appear more youthful-looking than usual. Her tanned legs were slender, and she accentuated them with white stiletto Manolo Blahniks. Yes,

Michelle was perfect as always. In my crumpled outfit next to her, I felt like a leftover on the bargain shelf of life.

"Hi, Cindy," she said casually. "I didn't know if you would show up or Jacques."

"It's my listing, Michelle. Of course I'd be here." My tone was like acid.

She stared at me sheepishly. "Look, I'm sorry about the clothes. But I like Darcy. She's a good kid. I thought she deserved to have them."

I pressed my lips together. "She's not your child, so it's really not for you to decide if she should have them or not. And I would have appreciated if you'd asked me first. Now I'm the bad guy in her eyes."

She sighed. "My apologies. I didn't mean to interfere. Now if you'll excuse me, I need to finish a few things for the movers. They'll be coming by this afternoon for the remaining items. I'll be leaving to meet Ben in Bermuda tonight."

Michelle turned to go back up the stairs, but I reached out and touched her arm. She whirled around in surprise.

"We're not finished," I said through clenched teeth.

A flicker of annoyance passed over her face. "Look, I said I was sorry. What else do you want?"

I fought hard to control the anger raging within me. "How dare you say those things to my daughter about Paul. Darcy never knew him, and it's not exactly like he has a chance to defend himself."

Michelle's face reddened. "Okay, Cindy. I know how fond you were of Paul, but maybe it's about time you let this crazy harebrained scheme of yours go."

I blew out a breath. "It's not crazy, and I think you know that too."

She frowned. "Whatever. He's been gone twenty-five years. If you want to waste your time on this so-called theory, that's your problem. But I won't have you making Ben upset about it. He feels guilty enough."

"Why does he feel guilty? Because he was always jealous of his brother? Or maybe because he had something to do with his death?"

Her emerald eyes shot daggers at me. "You really should watch what you say, *Mrs. York*. Perhaps you don't want this listing after all."

"You're under contract. You can't do anything about it unless you want to cancel the whole sale, and I really doubt you'd do that at this stage, *Mrs. Steadman.*"

She started to say something else but must have thought better of it. "You can let yourself out. Have Jacques call us after the closing next week. I'd prefer to not have to deal with you again."

"Likewise," I said, as she trotted up the stairs in her four-inch heels. My phone buzzed from my purse. "Yes," I said, in an irritated tone.

"Cindy?" Jacques worried voice floated through the line. "Why did you call me earlier? Is everything okay?"

"It's fine," I assured him. "The inspectors are outside now with the buyers and Tricia. I was just having a little chat with Michelle."

"Something's wrong. I can tell by your voice. Should I come over?"

I shook my head at the phone and tried to calm myself. "No. We had words. She said some things about Paul that were hurtful. And my car window was shattered last night. Definitely no accident." I told him about the note.

"Oh my God. It's the same person who did it before. Rachel."

"I'm not so sure." I then went on to fill him in about the call from Aaron last night. "She can't be the killer because she has a police record."

"Who else could have known about your car windshield back then?"

I tried to think. "Well, I think everyone knew. I couldn't afford to get it fixed right away and didn't have coverage. After a few days, Paul had someone repair it without even telling me. I was upset at first and wanted to pay him back, but he wouldn't let me."

"Cin, you should have called the police."

"I didn't want Helen or the kids to know what really happened. It's probably fixed by now, but I did take some pictures with my phone earlier. I'll go over to the station this afternoon."

"You should have called them last night when it happened. Look, you're going through so much right now. Let me come over."

"No. The inspectors should only be another hour or so. I can handle this on my own."

"Are they doing radon or just termite and structural?"

"Radon as well, but it hardly seems necessary. I can't foresee any problems. It looks like everything is a go, so stop worrying."

"I can't thank you enough for agreeing to take the listing," Jacques said quietly. "I know how difficult this has been for you. And that's why I want you to be a co-lister on that other mansion I landed yesterday."

I gasped. "You don't have to do that."

"Well, I want to. Um, have you—have you talked to Greg about, you know? Your little bundle of joy?"

"Not yet. When he comes home tonight." I sat down on the stairs. "Jacques, I'm scared."

His voice was soft. "Look, darling. It's not like you got yourself into this mess alone. Gregory will have to take his share of responsibility. Besides, he'll learn to love the idea in time. How about you? Are you feeling better about it now?"

I decided to be honest. "I want to be happy about the baby, but I just can't. God, I feel like a monster."

"I'm sure this is all normal. And in nine months—well, a little less—you're going to be a happy and proud mother. I know you. And Gregory will be a doting papa. I personally guarantee it."

"I hope you're right."

"Of course I am. Listen, you'd better get outside, and see what's going on. By the way, Tricia called me a little while ago and said you were behaving unprofessionally. What was that all about?"

"I wouldn't grovel at her feet."

"Good for you. I've got a client coming into the office around noon to sign some papers. Stop by when you're done, and we'll have lunch."

I really wanted a nap, not food. "Okay. I'll let you know when I can break away."

He disconnected, and I walked outside with a more optimistic attitude than I'd had before. Somehow, Jacques always succeeded in making me feel better about everything. Then again, that's what best friends were for. The world needed more people like him, and less of those like Tricia.

For the next hour or so I made small talk with the buyers and tried to avoid Tricia's hateful glare. Shortly after eleven, the inspectors printed a copy of the report for the Steadmans and one for the Whitakers. I exchanged good-byes and got ready to make my exit. Michelle had failed to reappear. I left her copy of the report on the folding table and made a hasty departure.

I sat in my mother-in-law's car for a minute, debating about what to do next. My phone buzzed, and I looked down at the screen. A chill ran through me when I saw who it was. Ben.

"Hello?"

"Hi, Cindy. I've been trying to phone Michelle, but she's not answering my calls. I was wondering how the inspections went."

"They went fine. You're free and clear," I said dryly.

"Is something wrong?"

"No. Where are you?"

"Bermuda. I just arrived this morning."

I tried to choose my words carefully. "Where were you yesterday morning?"

There was a beat of silence. "I had to fly to Florida to meet with a client. I told you this before. What's with the inquisition?"

"Remember Mildred, the nurse?"

"What about her?"

"She's dead, Ben. Someone strangled her to death."

He gasped on the other end of the line. "Oh my God, that's terrible. Was it a robbery? Who would do such a thing?"

"Well, that's what I'd like to know. When I went to see her, she said that Paul had something in his hand the day he was brought into the hospital. Remember how I told you about it?" Big mistake on my part. "Then Mildred called and said she remembered something. She wanted me to come over yesterday. But before we arrived, someone killed her. Kind of convenient, isn't it? Especially since you knew I was going to see her in the first place."

"Are you suggesting I had something to do with that poor woman's death? Who the hell do you think you are?"

"Well, what information did she have for me? She had a conversation with Paul about male sterility the day before he died. She said there was a name on a piece of paper in his hand. Whose name was it?"

"Maybe he did have a fling with Rachel," Ben said. "I don't understand why he would be talking to Mildred about something of such a personal nature. Did Paul think he couldn't father children?"

"Mildred said he had the mumps as a child."

"We both did. What does that have to do with anything?"

"I didn't know you had them too."

He ignored my statement. "Maybe Rachel came to him and

lied that she was knocked up. Who knows? He was acting really weird those last couple of days. I noticed it when I came to the hospital for my test earlier that week."

"What type of test?"

He paused. "Um, Paul was aware I needed money and said he knew of a clinic that was paying top dollar for—you know… male donations."

"What are you talking about?"

"Come on Cindy. Don't make me spell it out for you. You know. Women that wanted children but needed a little help in making them. Now do you get it?"

Ew. "No offense but why would *you* need the money? Your family was rich."

His voice was low, almost monotone. "I needed it more than you might think. I had a bit of a gambling problem back then. I'd just returned from a weekend in Vegas where I'd squandered ten grand. My father was furious and cut me off for a while. So this seemed like a good idea—you know, an easy way to get cash. I was hesitant, but when I got to the hospital Paul gave me a vial and assured me he'd take care of everything else. Said he'd bring it to the clinic himself and then let me know how to go about getting my money. Turns out, I never did get paid for the sample. When he died, I forgot all about it. Maybe he never got a chance to turn it in."

Something here wasn't adding up. "This makes no sense. I can't picture Paul asking you for a—um, specimen. Was he a donor too? Is that how he found out he was sterile?"

"I have no idea. He never mentioned that to me. But as you know, he was going to medical school, so I'm sure he needed cash too."

"But Paul wasn't a doctor. Why would you let him arrange all of this? Didn't it seem fishy to you?"

His voice was defensive. "I was a kid and needed the money. How the hell would I know what he had access to or not? And I know what you're thinking. Paul's death worked out well for me. The prodigal son became the favorite one. My parents were so grief-stricken that I got everything I'd ever wanted. But I never would have hurt my own brother. I loved him. Honest to God."

I wanted to believe Ben but wasn't convinced. "I'm not ruling anyone out right now." Another thought crossed my mind, and the words poured out of my mouth before I could stop them. "How's Paula doing?"

"She's well, thanks. She's hoping to fly down next week to see us when we're settled in the condo."

"Ah. She's a beautiful girl, Ben. Looks just like her mother."

He chuckled. "I know. She's nothing like me."

"How come you guys never had any more children?"

There was a long, deafening silence on the other end of the phone. "It just never happened. I would have loved more, believe me, but it wasn't in the cards for us."

I clutched the phone tightly to my ear. "So, you and Michelle have no medical issues to speak of?"

His voice was so sharp it could have cut glass. "What are you implying, Cindy? Just spit it out."

Did I have the nerve to go through with this? "Ben, I'm wondering if you've ever considered the fact that Paula might not be your daughter."

Like an obscene caller, Ben's heavy breathing filled the phone. "You sick, twisted bitch."

I swallowed the bile that was rapidly rising in my throat. "I'm not saying this to be hurtful. But it does fit. Maybe that's why Paul wanted you to—to give a specimen. Maybe he suspected the baby wasn't yours. Paul loved experiments."

"Are you saying that Michelle might have slept with my brother? They never would have done something like that to me."

There was no turning back now. "She was carrying on with

Carl Williams about the same time that she was sleeping with you."

"You're a liar," he rasped out.

I started talking fast, afraid he might disconnect. "Paul caught them together. I'm sure he figured you wouldn't believe him, so he wanted some type of proof to show you that the baby might not be yours. Maybe Michelle was hoping to trap you with another man's baby. Did you ever have a paternity test done?"

The rage in his voice sent crystals of ice raining through my body. He muttered a four-letter obscenity at me. "You're way out of line. I want your name off the listing immediately."

"It's a little too late for that."

Ben swore again. "Your whole claim about helping Paul get justice is bull. You're jealous of my wife and trying to stir up trouble. Don't go near her, and don't step foot in our house ever again. We deal with Jacques from now on, or the deal is cancelled. We don't need the money that badly."

My stomach was waging World War III, but I continued. "I think you do. Especially since you had to hand over some serious bucks to that intern of yours because of the whole statutory-rape issue."

"I don't know where you get your stories from, but that's a lie too. And I won't hesitate to sue you for slander. Stay away from my family, unless you'd like something unfortunate to happen to yours."

I blew out a sharp breath. "I'm sorry, Ben. My only wish was to find out what really happened to Paul."

"You should be careful what you wish for, Cindy."

He disconnected without another word.

CHAPTER NINETEEN

I thought about going directly to the police station but decided to swing home first and check on the kids. Hopefully, I could also exchange my mother-in-law's car for my own, provided that the glass had been repaired. After I made sure everything was all right and changed my clothes, I'd ask Helen to stay a little longer while I headed over to chat with our city's finest about a case they weren't even aware still existed.

Did Ben kill his brother? Had he known for years that Paula might not be his child? Or had he been purposely kept in the dark? How would I learn the truth? It wasn't like I could force Paula, Ben, and Carl to all take paternity tests.

As I pulled into the driveway, thoughts turned to my own baby. With a sigh, I placed a hand over my stomach. How had I not seen the signs? And how was I going to tell Greg? I needed to lie down and think for a while.

As I went around the house and entered through the kitchen door, I noticed to my relief that my shattered windshield had been replaced. If I did have to go back out, at least I could use my own car now.

The twins were finishing up lunch in the kitchen, and Helen was at the sink washing dishes.

"Hi, Mom," Stevie said with his mouth full of peanut butter and jelly.

I walked over and kissed the top of his head and then rubbed Seth's affectionately.

"You look pretty bad, Mom," Seth remarked.

"Yeah, you're almost the color of the wicked witch," Stevie announced.

My color of choice lately.

Helen turned to give me a sly smile. "I'm sure your mother will be feeling better soon. In about nine months or so."

I sucked in a sharp breath. *Damn it. How the heck does she know?*

"I feel fine." I tried to pretend I hadn't heard her remark. "Um, where's your sister?"

My mother-in-law snorted. "Her boyfriend picked her up about a half an hour ago. Honestly, I can't believe you allow her to date at such a young age."

My mouth fell open. "Didn't Darcy tell you she's grounded?"

Helen whirled around, surprised, dish in hand. "She said you knew all about the boy coming over to take her to the movies. Brian something, right?"

"Ryan," Stevie and Seth shouted together.

I clenched my fists at my sides. "I can't believe she did that. But then again, she does a lot of things lately that I can't believe."

"You should throw all her clothes out the window," Seth said. "That'll teach her."

"She called me a geek this morning," Stevie added.

I hurried upstairs, wanting to see for myself. Sure enough, no Darcy. Something about this scenario felt off. I knew Darcy liked Ryan, but she wasn't gaga about him, like she'd been when they first started dating four months ago. Darcy was easily bored, and I was secretly relieved that she'd lost interest in him.

So why would she go out with Ryan now and risk being grounded for the rest of her teenage life?

Suddenly dizzy, I sat down on the edge of her bed. My life was spiraling out of control. The morning sickness—as with my other children—would probably soon become an all-day event for me. I was consumed with guilt about both Mildred and Paul's deaths. I couldn't seem to line up any new business or manage my rebellious teenage daughter. And now Ben was threatening to cancel the sale and sue me. Hey, everyone has problems, right?

Think. Try to focus.

I went back downstairs and found Stevie and Seth playing with Rusty in the living room and my mother-in-law cleaning out my fridge. I winced. "Helen, you don't have to do that."

She ignored my comment and kept wiping down shelves. "When are you due?"

I was thunderstruck. "Helen, I don't know what you're talking about."

She turned around to face me. "Cynthia, don't give me that bull. I knew as soon as I looked at you this morning. Plus, I heard you get sick. Have you told my son yet?"

Agitated, I pressed my lips together. "Please don't say anything to Greg. I haven't had a chance to tell him. I only found out yesterday."

For the first time I could ever remember, her angular face softened. "Having a baby at your age can be dangerous, you know."

She always knew just what to say to make me feel better. "It wasn't exactly planned."

"Obviously," Helen said tartly. "Well, it will be nice to have another baby to hold. And of course, he or she will have a wonderful father."

I waited, but she didn't continue. Nope, that was all I was getting. Still, an overall improvement for her.

"I'm going to find Darcy. Would you mind staying with the boys for a little while longer?"

Helen untied the spotless apron from around her waist. "Of course not. I love spending time with my grandsons. But I'd prefer to take them back to my house. I'm expecting the cable man this afternoon."

"That's fine. And thank you." It was times like this when I missed my own mother. It would have been nice if Helen could have been a substitute of sorts. When Greg had first proposed to me, I'd secretly hoped that Helen and I would have a close relationship—go shopping, bake together, share confidences. Then I'd met her, and my dreams had been squashed forever.

I started to reach out to her but stopped myself just in time. She looked at me oddly. "Is there a problem, Cynthia?"

I sighed. "No, nothing at all. I won't be long."

I grabbed my purse and got into my car. I called Darcy's cell, but she didn't answer. Big surprise there. I sent her a text. *Where are you?* No response. I sent another message. *You're in big trouble.* Nothing again. I tried to remain calm. Ryan was leaving for college soon. Could they have gone off to some sleazy motel? I didn't think Darcy would do something like that and debated about calling Greg. No. He was almost three hours away, and I didn't want to upset him. This was my problem to deal with for now.

I searched the contacts on my phone and found the number for Ryan's parents I had insisted Darcy give me on the night they attended prom. Ryan was a nice-looking boy with blond hair and amber-colored eyes who had a good future ahead of him. He'd been the quarterback on the high school football team, a straight-A student, but was also two years older than Darcy and leaving for Northwestern University in a couple of weeks.

I didn't want Darcy seriously involved with a boy at such a young age. I knew it drove Greg crazy whenever Ryan's name was mentioned, but I had convinced him not to say anything. If Darcy knew it bothered us, she would continue to see Ryan out of spite. Today was a different matter, though. I was going to ground her for the rest of the summer, maybe even her life.

No one answered at Ryan's house, so I left a message on the answering machine, asking for a callback as soon as possible. I lied and said it was urgent. I was so angry at my daughter for disobeying that I couldn't even see straight.

I drove down my street and onto the Thruway, getting off at the next exit. I continued down a bumpy, rural road for about a mile until I came to Pleasant Memories Cemetery. I drove through the open iron gates and parked my car on the entranceway.

I glanced around, but the place seemed deserted. The grounds were well maintained and several of the headstones bore flowers and a few assorted knickknacks such as American flags from the recent Fourth of July holiday. Although I hadn't been out here in almost ten years, I still remembered exactly where the family plot was. I walked down two rows and up another and found the massive bronze headstone that read *Steadman.*

They were all there, in a row. Paul and his parents, Arthur and Evelyn. I sank to my knees and placed my hands on the front of the smooth stone.

Paul Steadman. May 18, 1972 – June 20, 1990. Our ray of sunshine.

"I'm sorry," I whispered. "You didn't deserve to have your life stolen. You would have done wonderful things for so many people."

I traced my fingers over the letters of his name. I thought of the night he had kissed me. How we'd made fun of all the other couples necking at the prom. How he'd pick me up for school every morning after he'd gotten his license. The time he'd insisted on paying for my windshield and the countless nights

I'd come for dinner at his house. When we were younger, we'd always trick-or-treated together. He was the only male friend that my mother ever let sleep over when I was a teenager—on the couch, of course—while I remained in my room.

He'd had everything going for him. He was smart, good looking, and, of course, rich. I supposed he was a tad bit arrogant and all-knowing at times, although he'd never acted that way with me.

Who had killed my best friend? There was a woman who'd stalked him, claiming instead to love him. A jealous brother whose life had greatly improved when he was out of the way forever. A football player Paul had refused to help. And what exactly had Mildred known? That Paul couldn't father a child because of the mumps? What was I missing here?

I leaned my head against the stone and shut my eyes. "I wish you could talk to me. Give me some answers."

I knew in my heart he hadn't been involved with anyone else. It didn't make sense after his note to me. He wasn't cut from the same cloth as his brother. Had someone told him she was pregnant with his child, and he was trying to prove her wrong? And why had he lied to his brother about the whole specimen thing?

My thoughts shifted, and I found myself wondering what he'd be like if he was still alive today. Maybe he and Greg would have been good friends. I was certain he would have gone on to become a doctor, and most likely, he would have married. Or perhaps, as Greg had surmised the other night, I would have been his wife. I still had my doubts, but who knew what path my life would have taken if Paul had lived?

I speculated for a moment on how different my world would have been if I'd married Paul instead of Greg. Would we still have had twins or adopted children? It was weird thinking about a different type of lifestyle.

I wouldn't have been a real estate agent. Maybe I would have been another pampered, spoiled version of Michelle. I could just see us attending spinning classes together every morning and then lunching at the country club afterward. Or not…

Michelle.

What had she told Darcy? That Paul didn't know how to mind his own business. Is that why Paul had asked Ben to come in for a so-called donation? He'd suspected it might not be Ben's baby when he'd caught Michelle with Carl. He knew he couldn't tell Ben until the results came back confirming his suspicions because Ben wouldn't believe him.

Then I remembered the hat that Aaron had examined. I'd been so sure it would prove Rachel to be the killer. A blonde hair had been found, but Rachel had a criminal record, so there would have been a match.

Michelle, as far as I knew, did not have a criminal record.

The pieces quickly lined up in place, just like the Rubik's Cube Paul had always been obsessed with. Everything fit. Michelle was also the woman Doctor Sanchez had heard Paul arguing with the night before in the hospital. And Rachel had seen them together in the parking lot, talking the day before he died.

If Paul went to his brother with the test results, Ben would discover that Paula wasn't his child. It would have ruined all of Michelle's plans.

I flicked my eyes open and shielded them from the bright sunlight. I walked slowly and calmly back to my car, as if I had all the time in the world. My knees shook, but I knew what needed to be done now.

I dialed Jacques' number, and it went to voicemail. "I'm going out to the Steadman house. I'll wait for you on the side of the road, near the entrance. Please come as soon as you can." I didn't have the guts to confront Michelle all by myself. Although I was seething with anger at what she'd done to my friend, the truth of the situation didn't escape me. She'd already killed twice and wouldn't hesitate to do it again if necessary. I'd wait for Jacques to arrive, and then together we'd figure out what to do or maybe go directly to the police. I had no proof but still felt confident that I'd found Paul's killer.

I was about to put the phone away when it pinged that I had a new voicemail. I brought it to my ear and listened.

"Hi, Mrs. York. It's Ryan. Um, I guess you're probably looking for Darcy, but she's not with me. I mean, she was. But she just wanted me to give her a ride over to that fancy mansion where that lady lives. You know—the one who's been helping her with her cheers. I was going to wait, but she said the owner would give her a lift back home later. Hope that's okay. Bye."

The blood pounded loudly in my ears and throat until I was afraid I might suffocate. I threw the car into drive and placed a hand over my chest, trying to steady my rapid breathing as the reality dawned on me.

My daughter is with a killer.

There was a dump truck ahead of me, going about ten miles an hour on the rural road. I pushed the pedal to the floor and swerved to the left, passing him on the double line and barely missing a car coming in my direction. They laid on their horns and shouted obscenities, but I ignored them as my car continued to fly down the road. I had never driven so erratically before, but there was no time to waste. Darcy's life could be in danger.

"Please," I whispered. "Please don't let Michelle hurt her."

CHAPTER TWENTY

*a*s I pulled into the Steadman driveway, I tried to calm myself. Should I contact the police? No. I couldn't take the chance while my daughter was still in the house. I needed to get Darcy out of there first. *Get it together, Cin. Try to have a poker face.* Something I had never been good at.

My legs wobbled as I stepped out of the car, and my stomach began its usual rumble. I waited until the feeling passed. This was no time for morning sickness.

I knocked on the front door and waited. No answer. I knocked again. Still nothing. Was it possible they weren't there? Could they have gone to practice at one of the fields? I wasn't taking any chances. I reached in my purse for my eKEY device and synced it with the electronic lockbox on the front door.

The sparse furniture that had been in the house earlier that morning was gone. There were no signs of life anywhere, except for Michelle, casually leaning over the landing on the second floor.

The sight of her unnerved me. She had changed her outfit and was now wearing jean shorts and a low-cut, red T-shirt but looked a bit disheveled. Her overall appearance was different from earlier too. The perfectly made up face was devoid of makeup and strangely pale, as if she'd been crying. Her green eyes looked especially catlike as she glared at me.

"What are you doing here?" she snapped.

Crap. Had Ben called her? I managed a small smile and wave. "Hi, Michelle. I think I left my cell phone here this morning. Did you find it by chance?"

Her mouth turned up slightly at the corners. "No, I didn't."

I couldn't stand it any longer. "Where's Darcy? She has a dentist appointment, so I'm here to take her."

The smile turned into a full-fledged grin. "Oh, really? Funny, she didn't mention it to me." She jerked her thumb toward the hallway. "She's in the bathroom, changing. We were headed over to the football field to practice a few cheers before I take off. Looks like that won't happen now."

I fought to keep my voice steady. "I told Darcy she was grounded. She wasn't supposed to go anywhere. I'm sorry if she's bothering you."

Michelle tipped her head back and laughed. "She's not bothering me at all. As a matter of fact, it's perfect timing that she showed up when she did."

Alarm bells went off in my head as I stared at her.

Michelle returned my gaze, as if knowing my every thought. I forced myself to smile. "Can you call her? We really need to be on our way."

She folded her arms across her chest. "I'm afraid that won't be possible. Cindy, why couldn't you just leave well enough alone?"

"I don't know what you're talking about."

"Ben just called here and was very upset. He said you were making insinuations." Her nostrils flared as she continued to stare at me. "You have him doubting if Paula is his own child or not. Exactly where do you get your audacity from?"

"Um, he must have heard me wrong," I lied. "Why would I say something like that?"

"Thanks to you, he wants a paternity test. My marriage is over. I didn't think you were smart enough to put it all together, but you surprised me." She put her hands together and began a slow, mocking clap.

I prayed my face was not giving me away. "Michelle, Ben loves you. I'm sure you guys will work everything out. Have a safe trip. Now Darcy and I should go. If we're late, they'll charge us extra."

She didn't respond. Her gaze continued to lock on mine, and a trickle of sweat began to descend down my back.

"Darcy!" I shouted in a trembling voice. "We're late for our appointment. We need to leave *now*."

As if playing a role on stage, Darcy came out to the landing and stood beside Michelle. Two against one, with me being the potential enemy in their eyes.

"Hello, Mother."

"Darcy, we need to leave. Get your things. *Now*."

She tossed her head. "I know you're mad at me. I just wanted to say good-bye to Michelle. I don't care if you ground me again. It was so worth it."

Michelle placed her arm around my daughter's shoulders. "Oh, sweetie. I feel the same way."

Panic gripped me. "I'm not mad, Darcy. Please get your things this minute."

In resignation, Darcy waved at Michelle. "Sorry we couldn't practice. I knew my mother would show up and make a scene." She picked up her book bag and took a step in my direction, while she continued to glower at me.

Suddenly, Michelle produced a small, shiny, pearl-handled revolver from her shorts pocket and pointed it at my daughter's head. "Darcy, you need to stay here, sweetie. With me."

Darcy's face went pale as she stared down the barrel of the

gun and then looked helplessly at me. She mouthed one word.
"Mommy."

Dread that was as heavy as a sinking boulder swept through
my body. "Michelle, please. She has nothing to do with this. Let
her go."

Michelle reached out and pulled Darcy toward her. She kept
the gun positioned at the side of my daughter's head.

Darcy hiccupped back a sob. "Mommy, help me."

Anger and fear stirred within my gut. "Let her go. I'll stay
and do whatever you want. Just don't hurt my daughter."

She laughed. "No one would have known if it hadn't been for
that blasted time capsule. Who would have thought he'd leave
you a love letter? What did he ever see in you? You weren't even
in the Steadman league."

"He knew Paula wasn't Ben's baby, didn't he?" I asked gently
and took a couple of steps forward.

She pointed the gun at me but positioned her other hand so
that it was wrapped around Darcy's neck. "He was trying to ruin
everything. He asked me to meet him at the hospital where he
waved the test results at me. Somehow, he'd found out Ben
couldn't father a child. And he had the nerve to ask me if it was
Carl's baby because he'd caught us together a few weeks before.
He said he was going to tell Carl and Ben, unless I dropped my
claim that Ben was the father. He was such a smug bastard. Said
there wasn't a thing I could do about it."

Michelle's lower lip trembled as she went on. "Paul said I was
a gold digger. He was so vicious. I've always loved Ben. Maybe
he wasn't sure about me at first, but when he learned about the
baby, he changed his mind and asked me to marry him."

"Mom." Darcy started to cry.

"Michelle, I'm begging you. Let Darcy walk away and leave.
I'll stay here with you."

She continued on as if she hadn't heard my plea. "I knew he
was home alone that day. I was only going to threaten him. But

he started waving those damn results at me again. And then he called me a whore." Her lower lip trembled. "He said Ben would know everything that night. So I pulled the gun out and told him to hand the paper over. He refused, and the gun went off." She stared down at her hand for a minute. I attempted to send Darcy a message with my eyes to try to break away, but she was too panic-stricken to move. She kept looking at me and crying until I thought my heart would break.

"So it was an accident. See, I knew you never meant to hurt him." I prayed she would believe me.

Michelle nodded in reply, but I still wasn't positive my words were registering. She seemed to have retreated into her own little world. "And the old lady. If only she'd kept her stupid mouth shut."

I waited for her to go on, not taking my eyes from Darcy as I put my foot on the bottom step.

"I didn't want to hurt her either. But I had no choice. When I told her I was your sister, she was only too happy to let me in the door. I even wore a dark wig. That was kind of fun, going incognito. All she wanted was to chat and give me a cup of tea. Then I asked her what you guys had talked about. She rambled on, telling me she'd left you a phone message to come back. She remembered Ben's name had been on the piece of paper and that it had been some type of lab test. When I grabbed it out of Paul's hand that day it tore, but I didn't realize there was anything written on the other part. I positioned the gun in his other hand to make it look like a suicide and ran out of there as fast as I could. I should have been more careful, I guess. So you see, I couldn't let the old lady tell you. She had to go."

"Wh-what did you do to her?" I said in a voice that sounded strange to my own ears.

Michelle continued to calmly stroke Darcy's hair and didn't answer me for a moment. Darcy whimpered in return as I climbed another step. I had to pace myself, keep talking to

Michelle, and reassure her I only wanted to help. All I cared about right now was my daughter's safety.

"I had a scarf in my handbag and wrapped it around her neck. It all happened pretty quickly, and she didn't suffer much, so don't feel bad. She struggled a little bit at first, and then went still." Michelle shrugged, as if the whole situation was of no great consequence. "She was old and wouldn't have lasted much longer anyway. I basically did her a favor."

Darcy cried even louder. Michelle pointed the gun at her head again. "You need to stop, or I'll have to make you be quiet too, honey."

I was on the fourth step. Only about ten or more to go. My phone buzzed from my pocket, but there was no way I could answer it now. "Michelle, please let her go."

Michelle shook her head as she moved the gun away from Darcy and pointed it at me again. "I'd like to, but I have no choice. You know everything now. I guess I'll have to kill you both. I just have to think about what to do with the bodies."

I moved up another step. Darcy's face was a sheer picture of terror. She couldn't stop crying, and I was afraid that Michelle might do something to silence her. "Baby, don't cry. Everything will be fine."

Michelle shook her head. "That's close enough, Cindy."

"I'll help you get out of the country," I volunteered. "I'll go with you as a hostage. But let Darcy walk out of here. Come on, Michelle. Think about your own daughter."

I was only about ten feet away from them and thought about making a run at her but not with Darcy between us. It was too much of a risk to take.

Michelle stopped to think for a moment. "Maybe you're right. Why make her suffer. She's just a kid. I never really got to be a kid. I mean, I was a mother when I was eighteen. But I had to do whatever was necessary to hold onto Ben. My parents didn't have two nickels to rub together. Ben was my lifeline, just like Paul was yours."

For about the hundredth time this week I said, "No. We were friends. That's all." Boldly, I took another step.

She clicked the hammer on the gun. "I'm not going to tell you again."

I raised my hands in the air. "We can take your car. Let Darcy go. She can't drive. She'll have to stay here until someone comes for her. But at least I know she'll be safe." Truth was, Jacques would come sooner or later, and then Darcy would be with him. They might not get to me in time, but it was a chance I had to take. Darcy's safety was all that mattered.

At that moment, my stomach churned, and I thought about the helpless baby I was carrying and was instantly torn. How could I protect one child and not the other? Did I even have a choice here?

Michelle stopped to consider. "Well, okay. I'll let her walk down the stairs while you come up. But no funny stuff." She loosened her grip on Darcy. "Okay, honey. Start walking toward your mama." She kept the gun pointed at me.

I moved up another step. Darcy was only a few feet away, almost close enough for me to grab but not quite. If only I could snatch her, then flee down the stairs and out the front door. But I had already prepared myself to go in exchange for her.

"Mommy," she said in a choked voice and took another step toward me. "I'm so sorry. This is all my fault." Tears rolled down her cheeks.

I managed a smile. "It's all right, baby. Go on outside, and sit in my car until someone comes, okay?"

She nodded while Michelle continued to watch us. Darcy was almost at arm's length. I started to reach for her to pull her into my arms and heard Michelle laugh. "How stupid do you think I am?"

A cold tingle ran through me, and then I knew. *She's going to kill us both.*

I grabbed Darcy's arm and yanked her forward. "Run!" I ran toward Michelle. She fired the gun, missing me by mere inches. I reached her but stopped for a second to look back behind me. Darcy was at the bottom of the stairs, hesitating by the door.

"Get out of here now!" I screamed at my daughter.

The front door flew open, and Jacques stood there, gun poised in his hand. Michelle reached out and gave me a vicious shove. I reached for the railing, but it slipped through my grasp, and I was unable to stop myself from tumbling backward down the stairs.

I heard Darcy scream and a gun fire. My arms flailed out, trying to grab hold of something—anything—but I couldn't stop myself from rolling. I landed in a heap at the bottom of the staircase. I must have passed out for a minute because when I opened my eyes Jacques was holding my hand and bending over me.

"Thank God," he breathed. "You're okay, love. I've just called for an ambulance."

"Mommy." Darcy threw herself on top of me and sobbed. "I'm an awful daughter. You could have been killed. And it's all my fault."

I reached a hand up to stroke her hair. "Don't cry, honey. Everything's going to be okay. And I'm fine." To prove my point, I tried to raise myself into a sitting position, but a stab of pain shot up my left leg, and I yelped like a dog. I laid my head back down on the floor.

"My leg. I think it's broken."

Jacques glanced at Darcy. "Sweetheart, why don't you go outside and wait for the ambulance. We need someone to direct them. I'll stay right here with your mother."

"Daddy," she sobbed. "Someone has to call him. He needs to know."

Jacques exchanged glances with me. Then he got to his feet and put his arm around Darcy, leading her to the door. "I'll call your father. Don't worry, okay?"

She sniffled and looked at me for reassurance.

I managed to give her a thumbs up. "It's all good."

She shut the door quietly behind her.

Jacques came back to my side and grabbed my hand. "I heard you guys through the door. I suspected something was wrong when I got your message, so I brought my little trinket, just in case." His lips were compressed in a thin, firm line.

"You shot her?" I asked, almost incredulous.

He waved a hand to the top of the staircase, where Michelle's body lay. "She has a pulse. I got her in the chest. Unfortunately, I think she'll survive."

The sound of a siren could be heard in the distance as I glanced anxiously at my best friend. "Once again, you've saved my life. My hero."

He squeezed my hand. "You've finally gotten justice for your friend. You saved your daughter's life. A cold case for twenty-five years, Cin! One that no one even knew existed until you started poking around. So I beg to differ. *You're* the true hero, my darling. And you're right. Everything is fine now."

I smiled in return but didn't answer. Jacques seemed to have forgotten about one thing. In my attempt to save one child, I might have involuntarily hurt another.

Please let the baby be okay.

CHAPTER TWENTY-ONE

$\mathcal{T}$wo separate ambulances arrived shortly to transport Michelle and myself to the hospital. Jacques had been busy making phone calls to my mother-in-law, Greg, and even Aaron, who agreed to meet him at the police station where Jacques was wanted for questioning. Before Jacques left, he handed the phone to me so I could speak to Greg. The alarm in my husband's voice was unmistakable.

"Are you sure you're all right?"

Even though I wanted to, I couldn't tell him about the baby now. I'd have to wait until he reached the hospital, and we were alone. He was upset as it was. "I'll be fine as soon as you get here."

"I'm on my way right now." He exhaled a long breath. "Cin, you have to promise me you're going to stop putting your life in danger like this. I'm happy you found out the truth, for Paul's sake. But I couldn't live if something happened to you. I love you, baby."

My shoulders wracked with sobs. Again, I was consumed with guilt. Greg didn't know I hadn't just put my own self in danger. Another life was being threatened. A life that up until yesterday I hadn't known about and wasn't sure that I'd even wanted. Nothing could be further from the truth now.

"Sweetheart, don't cry. I'll be there as soon as I can."

I handed the phone back to Jacques. His face was sympathetic for he knew what I was thinking.

"I'm sure everything, er—everyone—will be fine, darling."

Darcy held my other hand as they transported me to the ambulance and looked up at him, confused. "Who do you mean? Michelle?"

He glanced from her to me, and I shook my head in warning.

"Uh, no, I wasn't talking about that psycho. Listen, sweetheart, you need to ride to the hospital with your mom. I have to go to the police station. I'll be back as soon as I can, and then I'll drive you over to your grandmother's house. Okay?"

She nodded and bowed her head. "Thanks, Uncle Jacques."

He reached over and lifted her chin in his hands. "Your mom is going to be fine. Stop blaming yourself."

Darcy rubbed her arms as if for warmth and smiled back at him but said nothing.

He gave me a kiss on the forehead. "I'll be back as soon as I can."

My lower lip trembled as I leaned forward to put my arms around him. "Thanks—for everything. I love you."

"And I you, dear."

As they were loading me into the ambulance, I heard Michelle screaming Ben's name. I'd almost forgotten about the both of them. I wondered what the police would say to Ben when they called him. To learn that your daughter had been fathered by someone else and your own wife had murdered your brother? I didn't know if this might end up affecting the house sale, but I couldn't worry about that right now. There were more important things to consider.

Darcy reached for my hand, while I laid the other one on my stomach.

She threw her arms around me. "Mom, I was a total jerk. I deserve to be grounded forever. You could have been killed. All because you were trying to save my sorry butt."

I patted her back reassuringly. "Don't beat yourself up about this. It's over and done with, but I can't promise you won't be grounded forever because you did disobey me. Darcy, you have to realize that when I ask you not to do something, it isn't because I'm being petty or mean. It's for your own good. I didn't know for sure that Michelle had killed Paul until today, but I did think there was something off about her and Ben, making them both untrustworthy. Despite what you think, I wasn't jealous of her."

She blinked back tears. "I should have listened. Michelle's a total loser. Who cares that she was rich, beautiful, and a big-time cheerleader. I mean, she *killed* people. Seth and Stevie are right. I am a moron."

I squeezed her hand. "No, you're not." If anything, I hoped that the experience would bring us closer. I would need to depend on Darcy in the future—more than she knew.

We rode in silence for the rest of the brief trip, both of us wracked with our own separate feelings of guilt.

When I arrived at the hospital, they made Darcy stay in the waiting area while I was transported into the emergency room.

"How bad is the pain?" The nurse wanted to know. She had short, white hair, a stocky build, and appeared to be in her late fifties. "On a scale of one to ten?"

I gritted my teeth. "An eleven." I reached out and grabbed her arm. "I—I'm not sure what I can have for medication. I'm seven weeks pregnant."

She glanced at me sharply and wrote something down on a chart. "Who's your primary?"

"Doctor Sanchez."

"It just so happens he's here, making his rounds. You had a pretty nasty fall, so we'll schedule an ultrasound right away.

Usually they're not done until eight weeks at the earliest, but in this case, it should be able to tell us if everything is okay with your little one. Any bleeding or cramps?"

"No, I don't think so." I continued to stare at her with my best pleading look. "Please tell me if the baby's okay. I *have* to know."

She patted my hand. "We're going to do everything we can. Once we see the flicker, we'll have a better idea."

I was puzzled. "Flicker?"

"The heartbeat, dear. I'm going to give you a little morphine for the pain. It's perfectly safe for the baby but will probably make you drowsy. Now, you just try to relax. Everything will be fine, young lady."

Within minutes, I found myself drifting off into a happy place as they rolled me into the technician's room. She moved the wand over my stomach and talked to me during the process. I nodded and tried desperately to stay awake but kept drifting in and out.

Then the words of the nurse floated back to me in my drug-induced haze. She'd called me young lady. I felt anything but young right now, but her words were a strange comfort. Perhaps having another child would keep us young for a while. I smiled at the thought then placed my hands over my stomach and drifted off to sleep, trying to imagine what this child would look like.

WHEN I OPENED MY EYES, Jacques was sitting by my bedside. I glanced around in confusion, not knowing what had happened at first. Then I remembered. I glanced down at my leg, which had been placed in a cast.

Jacques had been texting a message on his phone but looked

up immediately when I tried to move. "How are we feeling, love?"

I managed a smile. "It hurts, but I'll live. What time is it? Have you seen Greg yet?"

He shook his head and glanced at his watch. "He should be here any minute now. They brought you into a private room when I got here, which was over an hour ago. You've been out of it since then."

I yawned and struggled to sit up. "Where's Darcy?"

"I sent her down to the cafeteria to get something to eat a few minutes ago. As soon as Greg gets here, I'll take her over the river and through the woods—to the grandmother from hell's house we go."

I reached for his hand. "Did—did the doctor tell you anything? About the baby?"

He shook his head. "I haven't seen the doctor. And the nurse who came in wouldn't tell me anything because I'm not family. Don't you remember what they told you during the ultrasound?"

I wrinkled my nose. "No. I was in and out because of the damn medication they gave me. Find the doctor for me. I have to know that the baby is okay."

He smiled. "I knew your true maternal instincts would kick in before long. I can't believe that it actually took a whole day."

My eyes grew moist as I looked at him. "If anything's happened, I'll never forgive myself."

He kissed me on the forehead. "Stop worrying, and think positive. Psycho Michelle will live, but I'm sure she'll be going away for a long time, hopefully forever. Darcy gave me some bits and pieces of information, and I was able to fill in most of the gaps. How on earth did you ever know that Michelle was lying about Paula being Ben's child?"

"I didn't at first," I admitted. "But it seemed to fit. The hair that was found in Paul's hat was a clue. When Ben told me that

Paul had asked him to come to the hospital a few days earlier to give a—uh, specimen sample, the pieces started to come together. Paul was aware that his brother needed money, so he concocted the whole scheme to see if the baby really was Ben's."

Jacques grinned. "Pretty sneaky of him to plan that out. Sounds like we could have been good friends."

I smiled. "You would have liked him. Ben mentioned to me that he never heard anything back about the specimen and assumed Paul might not have turned it into the lab. Paul would have made an excellent doctor, but he was no shabby detective either. A regular dog with a bone. Once he suspected something, he didn't let anyone stand in his way until he learned the truth."

"So when the results came back, Paul found out Ben was sterile. That's why he'd had that discussion with Mildred—he'd been curious about what might have caused it." Jacques paused for a moment. "How did Michelle know about Mildred? We were out on the terrace that day when you mentioned her name. Do you think Ben told Michelle afterward?"

A light bulb clicked on in my head. "Actually, I think she might have overheard. Remember how Ben told us she was lying down because she didn't feel well? I looked up at their bedroom window, which was wide open. She must have found out that way." I laid back and closed my eyes. "Poor Mildred. Like Paul, she didn't deserve to have her life end like that."

"And your car windshield was smashed in an attempt to throw more suspicion on Rachel. All so that spoiled, pampered Michelle could keep her man and the expensive life she'd made for herself. Do you think Paula is Carl's kid?"

"I'd bet on it. He should be told that he might have a daughter and given an opportunity for a paternity test. I'll mention it to Aaron when I see him. I'd rather not be involved in this anymore, if possible. But if no one else wants to tell Carl, I will. The man has a right to know."

I bit into my lower lip and continued. "Paul had the lab results in his hand when Michelle came to the house that day. She claimed it was an accident. Then, after she killed him in a fit of rage, she made it look like he'd committed suicide."

"She never would have gotten away with it in this day and age," Jacques said. "Poor guy. If he hadn't left you that note, no one would have ever known. All he was trying to do was look out for his brother."

"A brother who was jealous and never even cared about him. Speaking of which, have you heard anything from Ben?"

"I ran into Aaron down at the police station. We chatted outside for a bit. He and an officer working the investigation are going to stop and see you later. He said the police had managed to reach Ben, and he was on his way back to New York." Jacques clucked his tongue. "Do you think he knew Paula wasn't his kid? Was he really that stupid to fall for Paul's scheme with the sperm sample?"

I shifted slightly, looking for a more comfortable position. There was none. "It's my guess that he believed Michelle right from the beginning. He didn't know about her and Carl, at least that's what he implied to me. I do feel a bit sorry for him. I mean, look what he's found out in the last few hours. His wife murdered his brother. He can't father children, and the daughter he thought was his actually belongs to another man."

"Yeah, talk about having a bad day," Jacques agreed.

I blew out a breath. "Michelle took Paul's life, and all because she didn't want him to expose her dirty little secret. It wasn't fair."

"I know, dear," Jacques said gently. "But at least now he can rest in peace. And maybe you can too, for the first time in twenty-five years."

I studied him. His green eyes were solemn as they observed me thoughtfully. He knew me well—too well. He drew a handkerchief out of his pocket, and I promptly burst into tears. He reached over and held me in his arms while I sobbed.

At first I wasn't sure what exactly I was crying for—Paul or the thought that I might have lost this baby. Probably a little of both.

"Come on, darling," he said. "Pull yourself together before Gregory gets here. You need to be strong when you give him the news."

I pressed a button on the side of the bed, and elevated the top portion at a more comfortable angle. "I don't feel strong. I'm still afraid to tell him, Jacques."

As if on cue, we heard footsteps running down the hall, and a second later, Greg appeared in the doorway. He looked awful. His curly hair was a disheveled mess, his face haggard, and he had circles under his eyes. Yet, still my adorable husband. For the first time ever, I was more scared than relieved to see him. He nodded to Jacques and then proceeded to wrap his arms around me.

"Sweetheart," he breathed. "I was so worried."

Showtime.

CHAPTER TWENTY-TWO

"*W*hat did the doctor say?" Greg smoothed the hair back from my face as he kissed me.

"I haven't seen him yet. But they did some tests, and my leg is definitely broken. They said it could take up to six weeks to heal." Thank goodness it wasn't six months because I'd be having contractions and toting crutches during a New York winter then.

Jacques rose to his feet. "I've got a call coming in. I'll be back in a few minutes." He winked and mouthed *Good luck* at me.

Greg sat down in the chair Jacques had vacated and pulled it closer to the bed. He reached for my hand and kissed it. "I'm lucky I didn't get a speeding ticket. I drove ninety all the way back here. Where's Darcy?"

"She's downstairs in the cafeteria. I'm sure she'll come back up in a few minutes."

"I can't believe it, Cin. Our daughter was alone with that psycho the other night. And she could have killed both of you today. Thank God Jacques showed up when he did." Greg blew out a long breath. "It seems Jacques is your knight in shining armor, not me. I'm never there when you need me. Plus, you haven't been feeling well lately, and all I've been thinking about are my own selfish needs."

My eyes filled as I watched the expression on his face. I couldn't stand to see him blame himself. "*You* are my knight. And it's not your fault you couldn't be here. You're a wonderful husband, provider, and *father*." I stressed the last word a bit.

Greg didn't seem to notice as he stroked my cheek. "Paul can rest easy now, thanks to you." He smiled. "Maybe you and Jacques should get out of the real estate business and open your own detective agency." He examined the cast on my left leg. "Although you're going to be out of commission for a while, Nancy Drew."

If he only knew. I blew out a sharp breath. The time had come. "Greg, you're—"

I didn't get a chance to finish my sentence because Jacques poked his head back in the room at that moment. He caught the hidden meaning behind my glare and started to retreat again. "Sorry."

Greg rose from the chair. "Come on, get in here." He reached for Jacques' hand and pulled him back into the room. "Once again, I owe you big time, my friend. What would we ever do without you?"

I sighed. At this rate, I'd be lucky if I got a chance to tell my husband before I delivered the baby.

Jacques smiled, and his eyes came to rest on me. "I'm afraid I have some bad news, my dear. Tricia Hudson texted me a few minutes ago."

Uh-oh. I leaned forward, trying hard not to panic. "She heard about Michelle, didn't she?"

Jacques' expression was grim. "Her buyers have canceled the contract."

"No." I thought I might burst into tears. "They can't do that."

He spoke gently. "You know that they can, dear. The contract is still in the attorney-approval stage. So they have the right. I guess the story made the midafternoon news too. Tricia saw it and called her buyers right away. Personally I can't stand the chick myself, but it was her obligation to inform her clients. As she suspected, they immediately wanted out of the contract. Tricia just emailed the documents over to me from their attorney's office."

I stared at the ceiling and sighed. "I was really counting on that money, Jacques. *Especially* now."

Greg reached for my hand again. "We'll be okay, baby. Don't worry. My boss is so pleased with my recent performance that I'm getting another raise next month."

It was hard to hide my disappointment. Once again, the big deal had slipped through my fingers. "Jacques, I'm not going to be able to show many houses during the next six weeks. I've got to have some income."

He nodded. "Remember, I told you I was making you co-lister on that other mansion of mine. You'll be taken care of, dear."

I shook my head vigorously. "I can't let you do that. That's your money. I wouldn't feel right about it."

Jacques tapped his fingers against his phone. "If it makes you feel better, I'll make a deal with you. Linda quit this morning. So I need a new receptionist, and you can't show houses for a while. If you agree to take over the phones until your leg is better and give me a chance to find someone else, I'll pay you Linda's salary. And you can still search For Sale by Owner listings, expired listings, etcetera. If you find a client who's interested, I can always show them the house for you, and we'll split the commission."

My lower lip trembled. "That's far too generous. You're really incredible."

He grinned. "Of course I am. But I happen to think you're incredible too."

Greg watched Jacques in admiration. "You're too good to us. Cindy couldn't ask for a better boss or friend."

I smiled. It wasn't too long ago that Greg had issues with Jacques and his personal life. I couldn't be prouder of him or my best friend right now.

"But we can still keep the listing, right?"

Jacques drew his eyebrows together. "Ben just called me. As you might guess, he was very cool on the phone. He's on his way back to New York at the moment. Given what he's just found out, I can understand his attitude. He did mention the first thing he was going to do when he got back was take a paternity test."

I closed my eyes for a moment. "What a mess this is."

"When I told him about the contract being cancelled, well, it was kind of like he didn't even care anymore. I mean, he has bigger fish to fry right now. A wife who's a murderer and lied to him about another man's child."

"So he may pull the house off the market."

Jacques shrugged. "Maybe. Does it really matter? That mansion is a pariah now. It won't fetch anywhere near the money it's supposed to. Everything's out in the open. The current owner killed someone there. You know how people around here think. No one's going to want it."

I sighed in defeat. "Another one bites the dust."

Jacques waved his hand impatiently. "Ah, I've got you covered. Until your next mansion comes in, that is. Then you can pay me back."

"It's a deal." I smiled but tried to shoot him a look of warning as well. "Hey, Jacques, would you mind—"

At that moment, the door opened, and Doctor Sanchez appeared, chart in hand. Greg stood up so that they could shake hands, and then he introduced the doctor to Jacques.

It was starting to feel like Grand Central Station in here. All I wanted was two minutes alone with my husband so I could tell him he was about to be a father again. I watched the doctor's face for signs that anything was wrong, but he smiled at me with encouragement.

"It was a clean break," he said. "I want to keep you overnight, though. And we'll get you a pair of crutches to go home with. In about six weeks, you should be good as new."

"Thanks, Doctor. Great to hear." I winked at him and gestured toward the door, hoping he'd get the hint and leave.

He stared at me, puzzled. "Is there something in your eye, Cindy?"

Unbelievable. "Doctor, I need to speak to my husband alone for a minute, if that's okay with you."

Jacques went to the door and held it open, hoping Doctor Sanchez would take the hint.

"Of course," Doctor Sanchez nodded. "But first I want to put your mind completely at ease. From everything we can see, it appears that the baby is fine."

Ugh. I wanted to smack my head against something hard. Then again, I think I would have preferred to smack Doctor Sanchez's head instead.

Greg looked from the doctor to me, confused. "Baby? What's he talking about?" Recognition slowly sank in, and an unmistakable look of panic crept into his eyes.

"Oh, crap," Jacques said miserably.

Doctor Sanchez's mouth dropped open in horror. "Oh, Cindy, I do apologize. I thought that Greg already—"

I leaned back against the pillow, defeated. "Doctor, could I have a moment alone with my husband, please?" *Even though the horse has already left the barn, thanks to you.*

Doctor Sanchez nodded meekly. "I'll—uh—stop by later." He couldn't leave the room fast enough. Jacques still held the door open for his departure, and from the look on his face, I worried he might push the doctor into the hallway.

Greg sat down heavily in the chair, his breathing shallow.

"Ba-baby? Whose baby?" His eyes darted from mine to Jacques' with alarm.

"Well, don't look at me," Jacques said defensively.

Greg whirled back around and locked eyes with me. "A baby?" he repeated.

Jacques cleared his throat. "Um, I'll go down to the cafeteria and find Darcy. I'll drop her off at Helen's and be back as soon as I can." He leaned over the bed to give me a perfunctory kiss on the cheek.

I whispered in his ear. "Please don't go."

He gave me a sympathetic look. "You two need to be alone and sort things out. I'll bring you back something to eat. This hospital food is the pits. What would you like? How about a nice mammoth-sized piece of strawberry cheesecake? I'll have Ed get one together for you."

"Thanks, but I really don't have much of an appetite." I watched my husband closely to see if he was still breathing. He appeared to be.

"I'll think of something special." Jacques gave me an encouraging smile and then glanced worriedly at Greg, who was sitting in the chair, staring dimly into space. It reminded me of my shocked response when I'd first learned the news yesterday.

Jacques opened the door, blew me a kiss, and then closed it soundlessly behind him.

We were finally alone. I bit into my lower lip, trying to be brave. I waited for some sort of reaction from my husband. He turned his head to meet my gaze again. I hadn't expected him to jump up and down with joy but secretly hoped he'd take the news better. After all, it wasn't like I'd planned this. I figured he must be in shock.

"How long have you known?" Greg's voice croaked.

There was a cold chill in the air, and I pulled the sheet around me. "Only since yesterday. I didn't want to tell you over the phone."

He nodded absently and fell silent again. I examined his face for any sign of emotion, but there was none. I was afraid I might burst into tears if he didn't say something else soon.

Finally, I couldn't stand it any longer. "How do you feel?"

His eyes locked on mine again. Still no response.

"Greg," I said in a tight voice. "Please be honest with me. I know we didn't plan on this happening. It was a total shock for me too. But I've got to know you're going to be okay with this. I need you to tell me how you really feel about this baby."

Greg was still silent as he reached for my hand and drew it to his lips, then placed his other one protectively on my stomach while I attempted to blink back tears.

His blue eyes shone as he smiled at me. "Grateful. For you both."

ABOUT THE AUTHOR

USA Today bestselling author Catherine lives in Upstate New York with a male dominated household that consists of her very patient husband, three sons, and several spoiled pets. She has wanted to be a writer since the age of eight when she wrote her own version of Cinderella (and fortunately Disney never sued). Catherine has a dual major in both English and Performing Arts. Her book, For Sale by Killer, won the 2019 Daphne du Maurier award for Mainstream Mystery/Suspense. She loves to read, bake and attend live theater performances.

ALSO BY CATHERINE BRUNS

Sign up for Catherine's monthly newsletter and receive a free ebook as a thank you!

Italian Chef Mysteries

Penne Dreadful

It Cannoli be Murder

The Enemy You Gnocchi

Cookies & Chance Mysteries

Tastes Like Murder

Baked to Death

Burned to a Crisp

Frosted with Revenge

Silenced by Sugar

Crumbled to Pieces

Sprinkled in Malice

Ginger Snapped to Death

Icing on the Casket

Knee Deep in Dough

Dessert is the Bomb

Cindy York Mysteries

Killer Transaction

Priced to Kill

For Sale by Killer

Aloha Lagoon Mysteries

Death of the Big Kahuna

Death of the Kona Man

Printed in Great Britain
by Amazon

76460999R00139